D1434168

THE
STONE
MIRROR

for THE PUTATIVE READER

THE
STONE
MIRROR

Ian Spring

First published 2021
by Rymour Books
45 Needless Road
PERTH
EH1 2JU

© Ian Spring 2021

ISBN 978-1-8384052-8-1

Cover design by Ian Spring
Printed and bound by
Imprint Digital
Seychelles Farm
Upton Pyne
Exeter

A CIP catalogue record for this book
is available from the British Library

All rights reserved. No part of this publication may be reproduced,
stored in a retrieval system, or transmitted, in any form or by
any means, electronic, mechanical, photocopying, recording
or otherwise, without the prior permission of the publishers.

'A hell of a book and such totally unexpected subject matter... This fiction is brilliant. As I proceed through the stories I begin to wonder which line of arcane, erudite, antiquarian, literary or religioso-psychogeographical learning this man is going to upturn and set on fire next.'

PETER FINCH

AUTHOR'S NOTE

(it is not necessary to read this)

Some time ago, enthused by an essay in some now defunct (Australian, I think) academic journal, I determined to write a portentuous (or perhaps pretentious) introduction to this little collection of fictions about 'metafiction' or 'fictocriticism': roughly described as that type of fiction which is 'a metadiscourse and the strategies of telling are the point of the writing', and employs lists, tables, spurious facts, parodies, mock quotations—blending essay and fiction, poetry and prose.

I intended to evoke Italo Calvino, Michel de Certeau, Georges Perec, Roland Barthes (the *lisible* and the *scriptible* text), Milorad Pavic, Walter Benjamin, *Tel Quel*, *McSweeney's*, etc. I even had some provocative quotes lined up:

> *Death is the sanction of everything the storyteller can tell. He has borrowed his authority from death.* (Benjamin)

> *Any new way of reading that goes against the matrix of time, which pulls us towards death, is a futile but honest effort to resist one's fate.* (Pavic)

Etcetera, etcetera… I also intended, in the best scholarly tradition to enumerate the sources for some of the more obscure literary references contained therein.*

That I have not done so (fortunately) can be credited to only one person, to whom I remain grateful.

To explain: the reason I was diverted from this path was due to a meeting with my (now) friend Simpson Grears. A couple of years ago, we were both tutors at the annual summer creative writing school at Tigh-ta-mara on the shores of Loch Awe—a grand Victorian castellated manor in the romantic style and also the home of Sgoil Chiùil na Gàidhealtachd, the centre for excellence in

Scottish traditional music.

It was a pleasant summer evening and tolerable to sit outside in the early evening until the midges forced us indoors to the sanctuary of the oak-panelled lounge with its colourful Jolomo paintings of crofts and sea scenes. We sat contentedly with a Caol Ila wafting its seashore nuances while the lilting sound of the young musicians practising next door contextualised the whole experience.

It had been a successful day. I had held a workshop on narrative and, primed by Perec's notion of a novel as a jigsaw puzzle, had encouraged my students to write down scenes on little cards and arrange them in Gerard Genette's categories of story and discourse time. It had gone tolerably well.

However, I was already anticipating my main piece for the next day, a provocative talk on one of the supposedly simplest (but often overlooked) questions of fictional composition—the naming of characters. Entitled 'The Hannibal Lecter Question' it provoked the students to question some assumptions: in the Thomas Harris novels, why is Hannibal Lecter called Hannibal Lecter? 'Lecter' is a typical writer's conceit, but 'Hannibal'? Did his parents somehow forecast that he would have a predeliction to cannibalism, or, on the contrary, did Lecter himself allow his unusual moniker, perhaps due to bullying at school, to lead him towards one of the rarest of human perversions or criminal acts? And (returning to directly address the students) did this appreciation then, upon consideration, prick the bubble of realism—the suspension of disbelief—underlying the narrative?

I was smugly satisfied with this speculation! I would then enlarge upon the topic: Ian Rankin's Rebus character's name is perhaps justified by its association with the real name of a Polish stage magician; but why does Louise Welsh name her detective novel protagonist Rilke? Is he descended from German poets?

At the school, one of my fellow tutors was the the crime novelist Simpson Grears and, intrigued by the complexity of his interlocking plots and the ingenuity of the conundrums posed in his stories, I hoped to have a chance to discourse with him on the theory of narrative fiction. This evening, however, I noticed that he was occupied, receiving the rapt attention of some of the students—notably the female enrolments on the course. Eventually, however, I found an opportunity to have a word

We exchanged some pleasantries and I outlined the narrative class I had delivered. I enquired whether he intended to analyse the narrative strategies of the detective story—perspective, the enigma structure, assumed knowledge, etcetera.

'Och, no', he said, 'I just talk about my characters. Where I found them, what they are like. How they relate to my own life and experience… '

'But as the assumed or putative author', I enquired, 'don't you stress the difference between yourself and your characters?'

'Not at all', he said, 'I tell them what they want to hear. Sometimes, of course, I have to use a little creative imagining!'

'You tell lies!' I blurted this out in surprise, although I really didn't intend to be offensive.

He looked me up and down curiously. 'We *are* writers of fiction. Isn't that what we are supposed to do?'

I really didn't know what to say, so, perhaps, I looked a little downcast. He gave me a little pat on the back. 'Look', he said, 'We write fictions trying to pretend that what we imagine is real. Why not, here in this wee retreat from the real world, don't we just carry on doing that?'

'But,' I added, 'surely there is a discrepancy. In detective fiction, no matter how hard you try to make the writing realistic, the denouement, when order is restored, must be fundamentally unrealistic.'

'Listen, kiddo,' he said, 'maybe we just let the readers worry about that for now, right!' He flashed me a smile and looked me straight in the eye as if exchanging a confidence.

'Right,' I said.

Most of the more attractive female students seemed to be gathered at the same table as Simpson Grears and I wondered why. I recognised a couple of them from my class and asked them how they were enjoying the school.

'Well enough,' said one of them, a buxom redheaded girl with a highland accent, 'But just now we're having a wee conversation with the cratur!'

Whiskies and a jug of water suddenly appeared and the conversation grew rather incautious and one of my students seemed to be engaging with Simpson Grears in a manner that I thought somewhat inappropriate considering he was a tutor. I felt marginalised and thought that I should engage in some way with the company so I told them about a short fiction I was in the process of writing about a hyper novel: a text manufactured by a machine —a machine, originally imagined by Calvino, that is constructed like a labyrinth and can tell all the possible stories in the world! I pointed out that (quoting the master) 'it will codify all human experience resulting in the disappearance of the imputed figure of the author: that anachronistic personage, the bearer of messages, the director of consciences… '

I thought this might interest some of the more perspicacious students but, to my surprise, they burst out laughing and, chastened, I excluded myself from the conversation until I took an early bed.

That more or less summarises my initial discussion with Simpson Grears and I will not detail to any greater extent the events of the summer school which proved intriguing although not without their repercussions.

When I returned home, I found that I was often reminded of that particular exchange at Tigh-ta-mara. At first I was resistant. However, on reflection, I decided that perhaps Grears's argument had some merit. So I edited the manuscript of this collection to excise the most obscure tropes, embedded quotations, references, etcetera. Then I sent the whole thing to Simpson Grears confident that he would appreciate the writerly qualities as well as the substance of the enclosed fiction. As a little joke (that I didn't expect to fool him), however, I attributed the whole thing to one of my more advanced students.

Needless to say, I was quite stunned by the response which came almost immediately:

'Dear Ian, I am concerned by the content of the manuscript received. Your student clearly has a dangerous pathological obsession with pain, death and loss. I suggest that they seek help before they harm themself in some way!'

He continued, ' ...as for the literary merit of the pieces themselves, they are no great shakes. Only two pieces could be classified as realist and they are short and unsatisfactory. Of the others; they revel in varying degrees of obscurity and at least one would be completely incomprehensible to the average reader. I also notice that one seems to be stolen from a volume published thirty-five years containing work by the noted writers George Mackay Brown and Iain Crichton Smith. But in general I applaud that, plagiarism is a pretty useful ploy for the aspiring writer.'

Well, that is that. I am not immune to criticism, especially of such a trenchant nature. So, after some thought, I decided that Simpson Grears was, at least partially, correct about the constitution of the volume that is now, unfortunately, presented to you.

It is a bad book (in every sense) and it owes nothing to anyone other than myself. To you, the reader, I do not recommend that you read it at all—but, if you must, do so cautiously and hurriedly, so that you can get on with other, more important, things in you life, and try, at least momentarily, to think a little kindly of the poor author.

* I don't think it is necessary, in retrospect, to mention or credit the writers I have stolen ideas off or have unsuccessfully attempted to emulate. I won't try to justify this is terms of pastiche, ironic extrapolation, meta-quotation, etcetera.

However, I suppose that they include: Peter Ackroyd, Donald Barthelme, Jorge Luis Borges, Richard Brautigan, Italo Calvino, Peter Carey, Angela Carter, Miguel de Cervantes, Andrew Crumey, Umberto Eco, Dave Eggers, Alasdair Gray, James Joyce, Milan Kundera, Andrew Miller, Charles Palliser, Milorad Pavic, Edgar Allen Poe, Alberto Manguel, Alan Spence, Jeanette Winterson, etcetera, etcetera...

According to Johannes Valentinus Andrea, on the islands of the Axa Delta (where wild horses procreate) the goodmen of Uqbar sought refuge from the purges and pogroms of unbelievers. To this day their obelisks remain and it is not uncommon to unearth their stone mirrors.

from *The Anglo-American Cyclopædia*, Vol XLVI (ND), p. 920.

But hurry, time meets us, and we are destroyed

Derek Jarman

CONTENTS

SHADOW

The ancient Greeks, baked in the harsh Aegean sun, believed that the shadow was attached to the feet. The folly of this view can be demonstrated to dissidents by making them stand on their hands over hot ashes; whereby it will be apparent that the shadow is, in fact, attached to the fingertips.

The Imperial Instructor

In the morning I was allowed briefly to speak to the spokesman for the Angels. His name was Suriel. He was short and thin, old and wrinkled. His eyes were lively but unfocused. Some glimmering sunshine revealed the sweat on his balding forehead. 'We do not understand why we have been brought here', he said, 'We are not Gypsies, we are not Yids or Homosexuals. We are not disloyal. We came peacefully in order only to obey the edicts of the Emperor...'

⧗

' ...We are not Barbarians,' said the Colonel, 'as you shall see'. In the afternoon I sat in the Colonel's office in a lumpy creaking swivel chair. Although the office was sectioned off from the same quarters that served the rest of the guards there was a pretence of comfort amongst the clutter. There was brandy and Madeira, and three or four cloudy cheap crystal glasses, the uneven stumps of their stems stained blood red. Along the timber walls were tacked agendas and bulletins and there were a few gilded frames containing sepia photographs of the Emperor's corporeal wealth on earth—giant citadels like domed breasts, phallic towers. The portals were supported by gigantic caryatids of bulky soldiers and workers, friezes were carved with knotted male bodies.

'However,' the Colonel continued, 'it is necessary to address the problem of the Angels. It is estimated by the auditors of the Emperor that there are over two million of their breed and their associated genotypes in the Empire. Due to miscegenation it is possible that the estimate may be over-cautious. We cannot afford to take chances. They are not all blue-eyed and uncircumcised. They do not work, they worship their own desultory gods and they are not obsequious to the Emperor.'

The Colonel poured us some brandy, offered me the glass and sat down solidly behind his desk, flexing his fingers on the green leather. 'We are not Barbarians, as I say. We do not use the women and children. We take only a few of the strongest of the subjects for experimentation and for the service of the officers. As you shall see, the removal of the aliery organs is only affected with a degree of care and compassion…'

The Colonel rose from behind his desk and surveyed the walls of the office, fingered a few yellowed papers and tested the dust on the framed prints. I drained the last of my glass. I already felt weary in this dim and musty place. 'You must understand,' he said, 'we do not underestimate the importance of your report. Nor must you underestimate the task that we undertake here. It is difficult, it is unpleasant, it is undignified. Daily we receive conflicting reports on the condition of the Emperor. It would be easy for the men to begin to doubt…' He was gazing intently into one of the deep recesses of shade in the sepia prints. 'Every step we take, every action we sanction, each observation we make is of vital consequence.' He turned to examine me intently. 'I am often reminded of one of the sayings of the Emperor—that a shadow never falls upon a wall without leaving a permanent trace.' I felt uncomfortable. There were dark shadows on the walls. I could see that the Colonel was a driven man, haunted by those shadows. I did not envy him—but neither did I envy myself my own task.

In the early evening, I took the chance to survey the camp, starting at the entrance, with its heavy gates adorned with unserifed capitals that spelled the name 'Arcady.'

In the yard there was a sundial, dialled with verdigris brass— the only artefact in the whole compound that was made of stone rather than timber. The inscription around its perimeter read 'we number none but sunny hours'.

I now determined to inspect the various sectors of the camp systematically—the Colonel had told me I was free to wander unimpeded and would not be questioned by any of his men. Set squarely around the central yard were the billets of the guards and the officers. To north and south of these, wired to the height of two men, were the compounds of the angels. Behind these and to the east were the baths, the surgery, the chimneys and the ovens. In one wired compound, on this chilly autumn evening, the guards were hosing down a group of angels. They were wide-eyed and shivering. The bodies were white and hairless. Some adults had dark blood-dried slots on their backs where the wings had been removed. I was surprised at how regular and rectangular the slots were; they did not seem to bear the stigma of human suffering. I saw a few young females, the rosy paps of their little breasts mirrored by the budding wings beneath their frail shoulders. I watched and shivered a little myself and I wondered if they were, as they seemed, oblivious to my gaze. I stood around for a while, just watching and almost expecting someone to challenge me— but I was undisturbed, seemingly not noticed by anyone.

Eventually, the guards began to herd the Angels back to their cells. The camp was quiet and still. As I stood, reluctant to move to my next destination, I saw a young woman with a lifeless face passing in the company of two officers. The sleeves of her tunic were frayed and torn and the neckline hung loose around one breast. She did not seem distressed and she moved with a great economy, almost as if she was floating along the ground.

I determined to move on and within a moment I was behind the billets where the guards were boiling wings in giant vats to make liquor. I had heard vaguely of this practice—for a purpose that was not clear to me—and I examined it more closely. In the vats, white bubbles surfaced among the brown scum which the guards skimmed off with long-handled ladles to preserve the purity. The odour was alternatively sweet and acrid. But round the rims and on the scorched ground there was a smell like burnt milk. I sniffed the singed air and I wondered what delicate arbitration of taste treasured such unlikely fare.

I was already weary and I had a moment, like déjà vu, in which the obvious realisation hit me that I was lost in a world that was similar to the world I was familiar with but yet completely different. It was a topsy-turvy world in which the rules and certainities by which we live had been replaced by others, more obscure and threatening. I longed to leave, to fly home to a simpler, more restful day. But I had been awarded this work, and I could not yet begin to question its importance.

The day had been long and I had not yet visited the surgery or the mortuary nor assessed disciplinary and emergency procedures. I resisted the temptation to curse those who had sought me out for this thankless task and continued. I inspected the surgical instruments with their peculiar terrifying beauty, audited the punishment regimes, recorded the suicides and deaths. I entered the ovens with their slimy red walls, sniffed the stinking kitchens and bent double to squeeze my tired body into the basement cells, and, eventually, my mind full of observations, half-facts, resolutions and questions, the day began to draw to its close.

⌛

We dined that night on thin claret and some chicken and rice. The chicken was pale, scraggy and tasteless. As time ticked on and the night grew colder and darker, the Colonel invited me to use his own billet for the night. The management of a reallocation compound, he assured me, was not only a daytime job; he had had his rest for the day when I was on my inspection tour and he would now be on duty in the laboratories until dawn. Before he departed I asked him one question, about the boiling of the wings.

He shrugged a little. 'You must understand that times are hard. Due to the Emperor's situation, funding for our work here is limited. We sell the substance. Some races favour it for certain supposed qualities…' He spread out his hands and raised his eyebows to indicate the question was of no further interest to him.

That night there was a storm. The rain descended in torrents and raked angularly through the fences and wires. I put my ear to the window and listened to the weather sounds. There was a hum in the background—like bagpipes or keening. I wondered if the Angels were singing. I wanted to rest both my body and my senses, but when I retired, I discovered that I could not sleep. I itched and scratched in the coarse horsehair blankets. I tried to lie on my back or my stomach, but found it impossible. Then, after some time, I subsided and, in a feverish dream, I imagined I was sinking deep into the sodden soil below the bunk. I sat bolt upright.

My nerves were agitated and my brain still jumbled from the last vestiges of sleep, but, after a moment, I began to perceive that I was not alone in the room! And then I sensed, rather than saw, a presence in the shadows by the door. As my eyes accustomed to the dark, the dim gleam from the perimeter lights permeating through the window revealed the tucks and curves of a face. It was Suriel, or, at least, a shadow or a shade of Suriel's form.

'I must speak with you,' he said. 'It is important that you know the truth. That your report dismisses nothing of our circumstances here.'

I did not ask how he had gained access to the billet, not wishing to compromise any additional information he could give me. 'I have seen for myself,' I said, 'the status of your people and the principles that are being applied to your reallocation. My report will be accurate and as complete as possible.'

'You may, however,' he said, 'be misled. We are not seeking any advantage from your presence here. We wish only that we are allowed to live our lives. We are not a proud people. Pride was the fault of Icarus and he fell. And when Icarus sank beneath the waves did the stir deviate the ships one inch from their chosen way? We ask for nothing more than the recognition of the Emperor and the opportunity to serve.'

'The Colonel believes,' I replied, 'that you *are* in thrall to the Emperor and that you are doing him a service as he is himself doing in his work here, which is unpleasant but necessary.'

'The Colonel is not necessarily a wicked man,' Suriel said, 'but he has deep fears that may be baseless. We are not a proud people, as I have said. Look at this village, everywhere it is open to the heavens. If what they said of our people was true—could any one of us remain harnessed to this sparse land?' I shrugged. 'You are a single man,' he said. 'Here we have families. We have children who wish to see a better future. I myself have a daughter. She has a fever. We bind her to her bed. Each night she cries out hæmr and dïrc, which are our words for hammer and nail. We dare not release her. I fear that unless there is some alleviation of our plight she will succumb.' He slumped. 'What can I do? Anything. I will do anything'.

I understood now that Suriel was not loyal, nor was he an honourable man like the Colonel, but he was, after all, human.

Then a peculiar thing happened as the rain lashed and the wind howled around the thin cabin walls. Suriel came towards me. I was still sitting on the edge of the bunk. He leant over me and whispered some words in his language that I half understood. I felt a weariness come over me and, before I could reply, I was lost in the black of the night.

I rose to a dun-coloured morning, but the hint of a dawn helped a little to clear the horrors of the night. My lips were thick and my eyes sticky. I tasted the bone and the chalk in my breakfast bread. However, after I had done a decent toilet I felt renewed and, surprisingly, when, shortly afterwards, the Colonel and I walked out, the day had cleared. After the storm the air was fresh and a slight frost made the grass give way slightly under each footfall. He took out a silver cigarette case and gave me a long thin slightly wrinkled and sweet cigarette. We smoked as we went along the wet way. It felt good.

I informed the Colonel that I had made some additional observations and obtained some new evidence that raised previously unarticulated concerns regarding the operation that should be incorporated into my report. I related my encounter with Suriel and the story he had told me.

'It is impossible that you have met with the spokesman', the Colonel said.

I was surprised. I enquired why he should think so. 'Suriel, as you may have gathered,' the Colonel said, 'was constant and loyal in his service to the Emperor. In light of the Emperor's reduced state he felt that the gift of his own life, given freely, might… might help retrieve the situation. It is an old tradition. Last night he took the decisive step.'

I felt like a small boy in the study of a stern parent. 'Then he is… deceased?' I enquired.

'Let us simply say,' the Colonel said, 'that the time came for him to pass into the clinical text of experts…'

'But,' I proclaimed, 'it is impossible. I saw him with my own eyes last night. My own ears heard him speak.'

'No, it is absolutely impossible', said the Colonel.

My understanding was beginning to falter. I thought my ears were turned to wax, a liquor swam over my eyes. When I eventually spoke, my voice had grown a beard. 'What, then, of the daughter? Is that true?'

'Indeed', the Colonel replied. Suriel does… *did* have a daughter. You saw her only yesterday. She follows the precepts of her father and attends competently upon the officers. She may make spokesman herself in her turn if we so determine.'

I did not know how to proceed, but, after a little time, I could only suggest that I relate the whole story in my report and let my superiors judge the matter.

The Colonel sighed. 'It is important that you do not,' he said. 'There are, unfortunately, matters that are more consequent; matters that I confess I have not previously fully disclosed to you. I feel I must do so now.'

⧗

The Colonel led me past the boiling vats into another compound. I followed obediently, still confused. A hut, smaller than the others with only grilled slats for windows, stood in one corner at some distance from the perimeter. He put his arm around my shoulder. I shifted uneasily. He led me to the grill and I had to strain on tiptoe to see in. Inside the hut were the most beautiful and perfectly-formed Angels I had ever seen. They stood lank-limbed or sat on wooden benches. They were blue-eyed. Their wings were fully formed and some were preening. They were hairless and naked. Their little members hung pink and loose. They were in the image of humans, but they were not so. They were unsized. One beautiful little homunculus had the perfect proportions and figure of a young man but was barely two-thirds the size of a normal human adult. As I observed him, he turned to face the window as if he sensed my gaze. His eyes were deep azure but inhumanly blank.

'Now you see the full horror,' said the Colonel. He came closer. 'They are diminishing. Who knows where it may end?'

I stepped back and shrugged off the Colonel's uncomfortable grip. 'Your report will vindicate our work here, will it not?' he asked.

I had dwelt too long in the realms of monsters. My muscles perceived an electric desire to move. But I did not. I wanted to escape. To dip my forehead in a cold shiny stone of water. To fly in the face of a bony wind. 'You have my absolute assurance,' I said. 'You will have my vindication and support in full for your essential work in favour of the Emperor.' I had a vision of hæmr and dïrc—hammer and nail. I did not know if I could feel pity.

I left via the western portal. The gates slammed shut behind me and I reminded myself that the original Arcadians copulated with goats. As I left behind the reallocation compound and its fulsome odours and rotting walls, I peeled off the suffocating khaki envelope that was my earthly uniform and my sweat-ridden wings blossomed and dried quickly in the morning sun. It would soon be time to deliver my report on the condition of the Angels.

As I ascended from the dusty ground and headed east towards the heavens above and beyond the plains, the air separated the filaments of my hair and my gums began to tingle as if they were receding as the teeth poked their way a little further through the enamel.

I rose slowly and gracefully on my way and the distant sun tickled my neck and my shadow raced along the fields of cereal and wet grass, grew fatter and then faded until it disappeared into the little grains of corn.

FAUSTIAN FICTIONS

I

It happened a little time ago. I was quite a success then. I met her at the launch of an exhibition of my paintings based on tragic historical moments: the Lisbon earthquake, the Holocaust, the Senghennydd mine disaster, the Irish famine, etcetera.

Now, it is fair to say that I have encountered beauty in many forms: the sapphire flash of a kingfisher in flight, the impossible speed of the fingers of the flamenco guitarist, the sweet scent of the dying rose as it gives up its bloom. But when I met Faustine she surpassed them all. She was small, dark. She had raven hair and white teeth and skin like silk. She was wearing lacy black underwear: a delicate transparent brassiere, long black stockings and suspenders and panties of gossamer slightness. The little black swirls of her stocking-tops capitalised her gracious legs perched on pedestals of stilettoed heels. I immediately invited her to share my studio and, almost before I had time to consider the situation we arranged a quick marriage.

The first while we spent together could only be described as an adventure.

'I will do anything for you', she said, 'I love you.'

I protested. 'It is impossible to love me,' I said, 'I pick my nose, I break wind regularly. I am unduly pedantic about domestic matters. I am culpable of wearing odd socks.'

'No matter,' she said, 'you have conjured me for your pleasure alone.' Her body sank into my own until each part of us became complete in a perfect pair. I had never known such blissful, inexhaustible pleasure.

Things continued in this vein for some time. Then one day I had a telephone call.

'Good morning, I am phoning on behalf of Mephisto Credit Services regarding an outstanding account in our lingerie department.'

'I am not aware that I have any continued indebtedness to you,' I said.

'According to our records, you have.' He briefly outlined the outstanding commitment and summarised the terms of the credit agreement.

'I'm afraid,' I said, 'that I am not prepared to concede such terms at the present time. The only alternative seems to be for you to retrieve the merchandise.'

⌛

Recently, Faustine seems to have changed. She sits for hours listening to trashy music, smoking menthol cigarettes and eating liqueur chocolates.

Sometimes she favours me and insists that we conjugate our bodies until I am on the point of exhaustion. At other times she screams and shrieks at me, derides my manhood, and probes my ego with low and dirty slights,

Lately, she has started to pick her nose, break wind, cavil regarding all domestic matters, and wear blood red stockings with scarlet rosettes. 'Remember,' she always says if I comment on her demeanour, 'I was solicited from darkness.'

I no longer wish to dream at night, but sometimes I have a fleeting image of a scourge of scorpions. I think this must be hell.

II

Some time ago now. It must have been two or three years, I think. I found myself in the tricky situation whereby I could no longer maintain myself as I wished and, due to some minor indiscretions and unfortunate coincidences, none of the usual credit agencies would consider my case. Therefore, one day, on the recommendation of friends, I discovered myself visiting a run-down basement office in a seamy street tucked between the business district and the theatres and taverns by the riverside.

A secretary received me at an enormous antiquated desk. She was small and dark with rouged lips. I briefly explained my requirements. She nodded without enthusiasm. 'If you wait in the ante-room, the underwriter will see you.'

I waited for some time, then the gentleman concerned entered via another door that seemed to lead from a staircase. He was of a darkish, probably eastern, complexion, dressed in a tight fitting grey suit and waistcoat. Although I am not tall, his head barely reached the level of my armpits.

'Have a seat', he said, and beckoned to a swivel chair situated by a small bow-fronted desk.

'I will not waste your time with the terms which, if you have read the literature provided, are already familiar to you. I am sure that they will be to your entire satisfaction. The only matter of consequence is the question of the security, which differs from that required by many of our rivals.'

He explained the nature of what was required in a rudimentary but graphic way. I nodded, knowing that I had no choice but to agree, and from the front drawer of the desk he produced the contract. Next, he took from the inside pocket of his jacket a small portable inkpot and a quill pen topped by a bright red plume.

I tried my best to sign but my hand was shaking and I botched it.

'Don't worry,' he said, 'most of our customers find the instrument hard to control,' at the same time blotting the signature with a little block of paper and sealing it in a parchment envelope.

'Now for the deposit', he said, and opened, behind me, the half door of a large oaken cupboard. From it he took the apparatus. It is difficult, now, to describe it—but it was large and resembled, as well as I can put it, a ship's wheel, except that it was divided into seven segments, each of which could be extracted on a bar or rail, and then pushed in again. It was polished and well maintained but looked antique, and, on each segment, in brass inlay, were symbols in a language I did not understand.

By extracting and then contracting four of the segments, he was able to fit the contraption over my head and then around my chest, tightly.

'Sit still', he said, 'there is no need for this to take very long'.

The handles of the wheel, it seemed, were fitted in a system of grooves on an outer track to the inner wheel, thus enabling them to be turned in increments whilst the whole thing remained tight around my body. Each of these handles could be unscrewed and replaced by an instrument like an eyeglass bent at a right angle around a reflector that enabled him to look down into each section of the wheel.

He adjusted the thing several times, each time re-fixing the viewer and peering into the depth. As he did so, he explained again, in basic terms, the nature of the operation.

'It is not essential for you to understand the technical details, but, for security, it is necessary for us to extract a small sample of a substance that you may like to think of as body fat from a section close to the heart. The extraction will be painless and we will only retain it until the final terms of your agreement have been met'.

When he seemed content with the placement, he removed the eyepiece and fixed, instead, a glass tube with a brass neck and screw top. Asking me to be still and breathe deeply, he turned this once counter-clockwise. There was a little whoosh like an escape of air and into the tube popped a white capsule of a fatty substance, less than an inch long. I felt nothing except a sudden emptiness of the stomach, as if I hadn't eaten for a long time.

⧗

It is difficult to explain how I subsequently felt. But it may be easier to understand if I confess that, for nearly all my adult life, I had suffered from a sort of nausea. This would usually occur whenever I left my home and ranged from just a slight sickly taste in my mouth to a feeling like a hand gripping the top part of my stomach. At its worst, when I was over-stressed or run-down, it would extend its grip outwards, across my chest to my arms, causing my hands to tremble.

After the operation, however, the nausea completely disappeared. I felt fit and healthy, and confident and complete. And with it came a new-found appetite. An appetite for good food, wines, female companionship, and the capacity to indulge in them as I saw fit.

In short, all that life could offer was now mine, to sample as I pleased, seemingly without conditions or restraints. This continued for some time until, one day, I happened to be passing and I returned to the office. When I confronted the secretary and explained that I wished to see the underwriter, she seemed genuinely surprised.

'Few customers return so soon', she said. She offered to fetch him. 'He's in the dead letter department', she said. 'You'd be surprised how much of our business is taken up in that way.'

I was shown into the ante-room and, after some time, the underwriter joined me. He looked a little anxious and worn. I explained that I was only there to congratulate him on his product which I was willing to endorse wholeheartedly. I would be quite happy, I explained, to extend the terms indefinitely, at his convenience.

'You don't want me to return your deposit then', he asked. I shook my head.

He sighed, 'Very few people do these days. Let me show you.'

He took me down the spiralling staircase from which he had first entered. At the bottom was the door of a large safe. He entered a three figure combination and opened the door.

I looked inside. It was dark but the interior was lit by something like a bed of gleaming red coals. On top of this sat a gigantic pile of what I assumed to be the little white samples that were extracted as securities. They were wriggling like maggots.

'I've been doing this for hundreds of years', he said. He gave me a sideways glance that was almost conspiratorial. 'I really don't know why I bother.'

We stood there, unsure what to say. He looked up at me and I looked down at him, our faces half lit in the red glow. For a moment, perhaps, both our hearts were filled with the weight of the world.

III

I met her at the launch of my third book. I was quite a success at that time. She was seduced by my autograph. I was seduced by her raven hair, flashing eyes and brilliant smile.

She said that she would like to enact some of the kinky sex scenes from my novels. I explained that such scenes were introduced for character development, dramatic effect and a hundred other pertinent reasons. I told her that it was an intentionalist and positivist error to confuse the author with his characters or creations and that, besides, the whole concept of authorship had come under attack from the most trenchant contemporary critics. She told me that she was too sophisticated and knowing a reader to make any such misjudgement of the situation and went ahead with the enterprise anyway. On the spot, so to say.

So we bought some handcuffs and gags, a ladderback chair, nipple clamps, a glass-topped table, etc. She applied herself to the business with admirable vigour and considerable skill— encouraging me to call into question some of the authorial assumptions that were plaguing my work and to seek to unpeel new layers of meaning from the fictional act.

Before long she had submitted her own modest first work of fiction to my agent. Her first novel was widely reviewed in the quality press. Interviews threw up some embarrassing revelations about our relationship and prompted accelerating sales

Meanwhile, I decided to stop writing altogether. It had occurred to me that the role of writing fiction was hopelessly gender-specific. The very act of language was a phallic intervention. I no longer desired or required the omniscient burden of authorship.

I had never thought that our affair was likely to last, but it has proved surprisingly resilient over the years. We hardly ever sleep together now. I sit in my bed in the morning with coffee and cigarettes and create even more kinky sex scenes which are not for dramatic effect or character development and will not be published.

IV

I had finished my penultimate ballad studies seminar of the session. We were discussing whether some classic ballads, such as *Edward* or *The Two Brothers,* were, in fact, subliminated incest ballads that had lost elements of their meaning over time. This fascinating topic was rendered quite meaningless, unfortunately, by the fact that only two students had bothered to attend, neither of whom were familiar with the relevant ballads. I decided to cancel the final seminar on infanticide and fraticide.

I was about to conclude when we were interrupted with raucous applause from the seminar room next door, scene of the penultimate seminar in Faustian Studies.

In the corridor, I took aside Professor Goodlad, chair of the newly established Research Institute in Faustian Studies. I was curious regarding the popularity of his classes.

'I'm afraid I can't take all the credit myself,' he said, 'we are fortunate to have been very generally sponsored by Dr Faust himself!'

'Dr Faust?' I queried

'Oh yes, rumours of his death are undoubtedly premature.' He winked at me in a peculiar way. 'In fact, he was here just the other week.'

'Dr Faust comes here, to this University?'

'Indeed. We expect him again next week. Instead of the final seminar we are hosting a lunch in the staff restaurant. You can meet him if you wish—after he has addressed the students. I'll arrange for it… but be careful,' he added as he turned to go, 'he's sure to try to sell you something!' He gave me another large wink and then he was gone.

One week later, in the bar in the senior common room, I was introduced to Dr Faust. His appearance was quite shocking, He was dressed shabbily for someone who could afford such a healthy endowment. Also, he looked extremely weary and impossibly old, his body sagging and his skin wrinkled and cracked. He was carrying quite heavy leather bound suitcases in either hand and a loaded framed khaki rucksack on his back.

I really didn't know what to say and the first thing that I blurted out sounded ridiculous. 'I always thought,' I said, 'that you had been torn apart by devils!'

He laughed, or rather croaked or wheezed a little. 'A common misconception!' He took me by the arm and looked directly in my eyes. I gagged a little at his sulphurous breath.

'You may have heard', he said, 'that I entered into a pact of sorts. That is true.' A distant and tired look flashed across his face. 'The result was not as sensational as reported. Think of it more as if I entered into a franchise of a type. I peddle some wares. I've been doing it for an eternity, or rather a little part of an eternity. They are actually the same as it happens.' His eyebrows knitted together and he looked either bewildered, bemused or in slight pain.

'Now,' he gestured with a short wave of his hand, 'would you like to see my merchandise?'

I nodded in agreement. I couldn't think of anything else to do.

'All the items are exactly the same price.' He said. 'You know full well what that is. What I have brought today are the most popular. This, for example...' He placed one of the large cases at my feet, 'is for those who lust after love.'

He opened the case and took out an instrument consisting mostly of a rectangular box. Then he explained how the instrument worked.

'There is a hole, as you can see, at one end. Into this is inserted the tumescent male member. The instrument then proceeds to lubricate it and caress it in unusual ways. At the same time a powerful sensor tunes into the brain waves of the subject, inducing fantasies of the most appropriate and gratifying kind. Finally, after the subject has had the most overwhelming and utmost gratification, the instrument severs the member at the root, anaesthetising and cauterising the wound at the same time—so that there is no pain, only pleasure.'

'Is that not a bit final,' I asked.

He shrugged. 'It is not for me to say. Each individual experiences it differently. Let me only add that many reviewers have praised its effects as a perfect metaphor for the human experience of love and marriage.' He shrugged. 'There is also a female version that performs a similar but opposite function. However, there is no need for me to demonstrate that at this time.'

Our eyes met for a moment. He obviously did not think I was tremendously impressed. 'OK.' He nodded sagely, 'Perhaps you would prefer to see the second instrument.' He placed the second case on the floor in front of him. 'It is for those who lust after power.'

He opened the case. In it was a large deep black bowl covered by a black canvas top. Pulling open a drawstring, he put both hands into the bowl and extracted a substance that looked like putty. He manipulated it in his fingers for just a moment. Amazingly, it took on the form of a perfect miniature white horse. He placed it on the floor and it galloped away.

'Using this instrument you can create your own world of which you are the sole master. It is hugely popular with those of a certain character.' He held out his hands like a conjuror delighted with his own skill.

'Be aware, however,' he added, 'that I am not personally empowered to offer omnipotence. When you have run out of new things to place in your world you may find that the clay forms itself into a miniature replica of yourself and you will then have to live in the world you have created.'

I was bemused by this. 'How many miniature worlds have been created then, and where are they all?'

He smiled. 'Who knows. Perhaps we are all creations in a little world imagined by some other lost soul. It is a perplexing concept. Quite postmodern, I've heard it said! Perhaps that is why it occasionally appeals to scholars, who I wouldn't always expect to lust for the material world quite so much.'

'Hmm,' I nodded. I could not disguise that I was somewhat impressed by his tricks. However, I decided, for now, to express a disinterested demeanour. 'Is that all you have to offer?' I asked.

'Oh no', he took the rucksack off his back. Perhaps our most popular product is for those who lust after knowledge.'

Perhaps I showed some surprise at this.

'Ah,' he said, 'maybe you expected something else?'

'Well,' I said, 'convention seems to suggest that what most people lust after is money.'

He chuckled a little and a sulphury odour escaped a little. 'Money! Cash! Kaboodles! Spondulicks!' He smiled, 'A secondary affectation invented by mortals'. He raised himself a little higher. 'I am proud to say that I remember a time when it did not exist. Believe it or not, mortals then were equally selfish, delusional and inept without it.'

He opened the rucksack and took something out. It was a sack of potatoes.

'What on earth do you do with those?' I said, astonished.

He gave me a look or either pity or contempt. 'You may do what you like, but most people eat them: boiled, roasted, sautéed, creamed—does it matter. I am here in the guise of a demon, not a chef!'

'And potatoes... *potatoes*...' I emphasised, 'ordinary potatoes give you the gift of knowledge!'

'Well,' he looked offended, 'not exactly ordinary... It was my own little idea. For centuries the apple was a symbol of forbidden knowledge. I substituted the humble pomme de terre—a more earthy and patrician symbol.'

'OK,' I raised my hand, 'what exactly will these humble spuds tell me, then?'

He snorted in a show of exasperation. 'And how should I know? Is light wrapped around the universe? What is the true condition of the human heart? Anything, but presumably what you need to know.'

I thought for a moment that his attitude was both supercilious and partronising. 'Yes, well perhaps,' I said. 'Maybe they will tell me that what I need to know is that you are a phoney and a trickster and a liar!'

He wilted a little at this attack and then, it seemed, a few genuine tears came to his eyes.

'There is no need to get personal,' he said, 'I am simply doing my job. If you are not satisfied with what I have shown you, I can retrieve more merchandise from the warehouse. There is a limit to what I can carry at my age.' His shoulders slumped and he seemed to shrink into himself. I felt the weariness of his old bones sink into my own body.

I felt more sympathetic now. 'No, no, old man. You sit here and have a rest.'

Some opportunities come only once a lifetime. I considered briefly and made my choice. I now wish that I had considered at greater length.

V

It was after the publication of my first two novels. I was quite a success at that time. I was sitting at my desk with my laptop and a glass of claret contemplating my next work. My third novel, I'm afraid to say, was quite essential to my continued wellbeing and financial stability. Nevertheless, for some time I had been aware that I hadn't the faintest idea what it would be about.

So, once again, on a grey afternoon, I was staring motionless at the computer screen wishing for a relief to this cursed impasse when, suddenly, for no apparent reason, the desktop display seemed to become misty and white. I rubbed my eyes. Clouds seemed to be forming and shifting in front of me and I thought that I could almost detect shapes, maybe faces, behind the mist. Then, as I leaned towards the screen, there was a tapping noise, as if something inside the monitor was trying to attract my attention. I jumped back in shock. My chair fell over. I ran to the window and pulled aside the net curtain. Outside, the street seemed busy enough, some cars and vans went by and pedestrians pushed baby buggies and raised umbrellas against the spitting rain.

I skirted the room—avoiding the desk—and went to the bathroom and splashed water on my eyes. Then I went to the kitchen. Only three bottles remained in the case of bordeaux I had bought earlier that week. I wasn't sure whether this acknowledgment triggered relief or despair. Then the doorbell rang.

At the door was a small, square-shaped gentleman dressed in a faded garberdine coat, tackety boots, fingerless mittens and a leather hat with giant earflaps. Although he was barely five feet tall, his face seemed impossibly large for his body. It was well worn, pale with tufts of greyish hair. His lips were thin and red, his eyebrows shaggy and his eyes bulbous and watery. He was carrying a large battered suitcase.

Before I had time to say anything, he had adroitly stepped past me into the hall and was peering into my study.

'Excuse me,' I said, 'who are you?'

'Och,' he said, 'I go by various names. Don't concern yourself about that.'

He headed into my study towards the desk. 'Don't worry,' he said, 'It's quite a simple job. Just spare me some of your time and we'll soon have you set up and running.'

Before I knew it he had shut the lid on my laptop and cleared a space on the desk.

'Hold on,' I said, ' I don't recall ordering any new equipment.'

'Hmm.' He barely cast a glance at me. 'There is no doubt about what *you* need. One of these…'

Almost in one movement, he opened his suitcase and took out an object. It was clearly some sort of computer, but small and compact with a round case and screen and a compact flip-out keyboard. It was completely white, with only an indent to distinguish the symbols on the keyboard. He placed it on the desk.

I stared at it. He looked at me for the first time fully in the face. 'I can see that you are a man of discretion. You appreciate a fine piece of stylish design,' he said.

'What is it?' I enquired.

'Och, don't think too much about that. Some people call it the mimesis machine. But you should just think of it as very like an ordinary desktop computer.'

'It's very… very white!' I couldn't think of anything else to say.

'Well, yes. Most of what I have always dealt in is white, the colour of death. In the old days, things were much simpler: the tiny skull of an angel, the bleached bones of a saint, a stuffed albino rat. Now everyone wants so much more!'

He pressed a button and the object lit up, a translucent glow lighting it from within. 'Wireless!' he said, and gave out a small hoarse laugh. 'Not *a* wireless—wireless, transistor radio, ghetto blaster, walkman, music centre, stereo, home cinema, wi-fi. Pah. Nine hundred years old and I've had all that technology to discover in just a few decades!'

At this point he stopped and smiled and nodded slightly. 'Ah, Well. I suppose I must take part of the blame... Guglielmo Marconi, such an ambitious boy. I couldn't grudge him a little success.'

I stared at him. His face was pock-marked and blotchy, his skin almost transparent. He was twitching. I could have sworn that shapes seemed to move below the surface of his brow and his cheeks.

'Ah, you are concerned about my complexion, I see.' He ran his fingers down his cheekbones. 'I was boiled in oil during the Gregorian inquisition. I'm afraid it has never been the same since.'

He turned away from me and waved his hand towards the screen in a flamboyant gesture. 'Now, *voila...*'

The screen of the machine was plain white. In large grey letters it simply said 'Please select your choice: 1. novel; 2 poem; 3 play.'

'Go ahead,' he said.

Somehow I was fascinated. I reached out and discerned the indented shape of a '1' on the keyboard. I pressed it. The screen changed to 'Please wait: processing.'

'What do we do now?' I asked him.

He shrugged. 'Let's sit and wait. I could do with a rest—four continents in one day, and at my age!'

'Coffee, please,' he added, 'no milk, five sugar. Coffee, 'hot as hell, black as the devil' as my good friend Talleyrand used to say —after the Terror, you know.'

⧗

We had coffee and Earl Grey tea. We sat in silence. When the visitor sipped his coffee, I noticed that his face grew pinker, then the colour seemed to fade away from the top downwards, as if sinking into some pit. After a few minutes the machine made a beeping sound. I looked at the screen. It now read as follows:

Title: *Expense of Spirit*

Synopsis:
M, a successful academic, is recovering from the loss of a lover.
M meets D, a young poet.
M is fascinated by D's effortless genius.
M falls in love with D.
D betrays M.
M decides to kill himself.
M kills D instead.
M discovers that he now has the gift of poetry.

First paragraph:
Why is it that so many men of talent or even genius succumb to that not uncommon affliction that draws them to the one ambition that they find hardest to achieve. For the first time in his life, Michael felt a twinge of regret; his personal sun had risen its height and been eclipsed.

As I was gazing at the screen, the telephone rang. 'Ah,' said the visitor, 'that may be your publisher. Phoning to congratulate you on your new work.' I looked at him queerly.

'Time distortion. Never really understood it myself. Had a few conversations with my friend Al back in the 20s, mind you.'

The next year or so went quickly and comfortably. The reviews of my new work were good: 'a new direction for the author, but handled with both subtlety and passion... '; 'a sort of magic realism; but a very terse British protestant type that pulls no punches...'

I stopped drinking, bought a new wardrobe, made sure I was often seen at the city's most fashionable venues (since I didn't actually have to write any more, my time was largely available). I told myself that I deserved this time. That it would allow me to reflect, to develop new ideas, a new life.

The next novel, *Waste of Shame*, was even more of a success than its predecessor. The reviewers were ecstatic. There was even talk of the Booker Prize. I was invited to more readings, openings and literary parties than I could possibly attend.

Things went along in this fashion for a time. However, the third work produced by my authorial machine, *Old Woes, New Wail*, caused me some concern. I was perplexed to discover that the name of its protagonist, for some unknown reason, resembled my own—in fact, it differed in only one letter. I instructed my publisher that all incidents of the name 'Masterston' in the novel were to be changed to 'McBeath', and sat back to await the reviews.

However, when they arrived they were almost universally disappointing: 'this novel simply loses its way before it is even half read... '; 'an ineffectual hero, a confusing denouement. Are these the ravings of an author in terminal decline?'

Undoubtedly, this criticism disturbed me, but I sat back and rationally evaluated the situation. All novelists, I considered, occasionally produced a work that failed to meet the standard of the others. Critics liked nothing better than to pounce on a failure from a successful and prosperous writer. It had happened before—to Orwell, to Amis, to Gray. I decided that I should consider this just a blip on my progression in the writing world that would soon be resolved and forgotten.

I decided—after a few weeks mulling this over—that I would move on and produce another work that, I fervently hoped, would only consolidate my reputation. I turned on the machine. I stared at the white screen until some text appeared

Title: *Onlie Begetter*

Synopsis:
M is determined to be a successful author.
M discovers a magical machine to do his dirty work.
M is exposed as a fraud.
M is alone
M destroys himself by poisoning.
M has no other choice.

I looked in the mirror, something I realised I had not done for some time. The result was not satisfactory. My visage was drained of blood reflecting the ghastly white of the machine. I seemed to have grown older. My face was larger, more jowly. My eyebrows were uneven, wiry white hairs protruded from tufts above my ears.

Almost in a trance, in seek of some solace and reassurance, I took one of my own books from the shelf. When I opened it, however, the words flew from the pages like a covey of birds flushed from the undergrowth. I stared at the blank empty paper. A little voice began to repeat itself inside my head. 'Is this all that you are worth?' it said.

I sat alone until the sun set, the same words echoing in my head. I imagined I could feel my bones settling in the chair, my body shrinking and ageing around me.

Eventually, after minutes or hours or days, I went to the kitchen. The remaining untouched bottles of bordeaux from a year or more past seemed to have exploded, leaving the floor a sticky blood red. The coffee was waiting for me. No milk, five sugars. Black as the Devil. Hot as Hell.

SPIRITS OF AIR, SPIRITS OF WATER, SPIRITS OF STONE

Calenture (kæ.lĕntiuer), *sb,*

1a. A disease incident to sailors within the tropics, characterised by delirium in which the patient, it is said, fancies the sea to be green fields and wishes to leap into it.

1593 NASHE *Christ's T.* (1613) 92 Then (as if possessed with the Calentura) thou shalt offer to leape.

1721 SWIFT *S. Sea Proj.* v11, So, by a calenture misled, The mariner with rapture sees, On the smooth ocean's azure bed, Enamell'd fields and verdant trees.

1804 GOODLAD *Legend and Lore of the Northern Isles* I, 34 The callant, possessed of a calenture, threw himself into the stony black mirror of the ocean.

1841 HOR. SMITH *Moneyed Man* III. ix. 238 The mirage of a calenture, which conjures up unexisting objects.

There is an old story that can be found in Chinese literature of the eight and ninth centuries, in *The Arabian Nights*, the thirteenth-century *Cantigas de Santa Maria* of Alfonso X of Castile, the *Cent Nouvelles Novelles* and also in Tulloch's *Old Lore of the Hebrides and Northern Isles*. It concerns a sailor who sets off to sea. We can imagine him as swarthy and dark or pasty-faced; a Viking or a Basque. He may be wearing a neckerchief, a dungaree jacket or a blackball hat. Perhaps his hair is tarred in a pigtail, his ear pierced by a single gold ring which would pay for his burial, or allow Neptune to fish him from the brine with his trident. He may be familiar with the embarcaderos of Valparaiso, New Bedford or the Barbary Coast, with pulperias and groggeries, fandango-houses and cantinas, or he may be a young arab street trader or Scottish crofter at sea for the first time.

However we imagine our sailor he will again encounter the

vast oceans as if for the first time. Silvery or sunless, Homeric wine or Cimmerian ink. He will stare into the infinity of sea and detect, on the margins of consciousness, the shadows of enormous creatures below the waves. He will see faces in the foam which he will eventually reconcile to a reflection of his own countenance, or at least his appearance as he imagined it on shore. (At times he may whisper his name to himself to remind him of the boy he left behind).

All of those adrift on the oceans dream vivid dreams. As they get farther and farther from shore these dreams intensify. They are the only vestige that remains of the land, the community left behind. Our sailor will dream of golden temples, flying serpents, the sea as a mountain and fire like ice. If he is in a fever from too much salt horse and sour water he will start to dream of a home port of alleys and wynds and taverns with hot rum and cold milk. Little by little, he will dream the cobblestones, the lime-plastered walls, the panes of flowing glass until the dream becomes as real as his own home which has inexorably receded into the distance.

No voyage lasts forever. The ship finds port in a foreign land. The sailor leaves the silence of the sea, wanders the streets of the town or city and is swallowed by the noise and bustle. He is surprised to find that some features, say the tap water running in the gutters or the oak barrels in a particular tavern, are identical to those of his dream. Others are more alien and mystifying.

After a while, the sailor comes to know the city and its ways. Although he knows only the spirits of water that have tormented him, old men tell him of spirits of air whose voices are hidden in your own belches and farts and who live in boiling water and bedclothes and in the creases and curves of your own body; and of the spirits of stone who can only move freely below ground and freeze solid in the open air. These stories trouble him as he wanders the streets.

He comes across old graveyards where the sandstone swells and flakes below the inscriptions and tendrils of ivy prod into the folds and tucks of mausoleums. He imagines himself as a soft sullen child or as a wasted old man slipping into the sorry turf sod. The land sucks him down as mercilessly as the sea. Frightened he hurries away.

Eventually, in a panic, lost in the strangeness of a foreign place, he determines to find his way back to his ship, the only link with the world he once knew. Running from street to alley to lane, eventually, with an effort of will, he closes his eyes in a frenzy and, as if awakening from a dream, exits a narrow alley to see the quayside walls and buildings. There are massing clouds in the sky and, above, the perfect loop of a scavenging seagull. Ahead of him, however, there is no mast or sail of the whaler or sandalwood trader from which he once disembarked. The ship has gone and the sailor's life has been subsumed into narrative.

This is the ultimate country,
This is the final shore.
They'll haunt you like a mirror,
The streets you've walked before.

No ship awaits your boarding,
Here you will grow grey and old.
Your life is wasted in this harbour,
And now throughout the world.

The sailor is locked in the labyrinth of his own life. As a coda to this story we may imagine that the sailor comes across a magician who offers him a choice. He can exit from his house by two doors. One is a portal to the life he has dreamt for himself; the other the life that might have been. The magician can only answer one question about the doors. The sailor must point at one door and ask the question. However, the magician must lie if he points to the door that leads to the dreamt life and tell the truth if he points to the other.

The sailor is wise to this horny old trick. He points to the left hand door and asks the magician: 'if I pointed to the other door, would you tell me that it leads to the life I have dreamed?'

The magician answers the sailor and he exits by the left hand door. He wanders the streets of a city that seems familiar. He smells cinnamon and foul water. He hears the yelping of a mangy dog. Through the window of a dosshouse he sees a beggar give birth. The woman's belly, pulled taut, is suddenly released and falls flat, like a canvas sail when the wind drops. The ancient city is too old for him now. The old wine has broken the new bottles. The pavements roll around each footstep feeling the tenor of his reluctant return.

He comes upon some lumpy statues above inscriptions in a language he cannot read. He imagines they are spirits of stone. He wonders if, at some glacial speed unseen to him, they are laughing or mouthing or spitting.

He imagines that he might die. He sees his own eyelashes flutter away like dandelion seeds, the filaments of hair snap and arch to the soil like spears, on the paving rattles a small pile of finger and toenails. Skin peels from the stone as the clouds race across the sky. He feels his own shadow in the mirror of stone.

He does not die. He is as green as grass and, eventually, he returns to the same house he has left and there he discovers the magician and the two doors still awaiting him.

FAQs

Q Is death inevitable?

A I think I can put your mind at rest here. There is absolutely NO concrete evidence that death is inevitable. Certainly, there have been observed examples of the physical decay and eventual failure of the human form. These have increased over the years. For example, Adam and Eve had not an inkling that death even existed! (At least not until Cain did away with Abel). Today, as the birth rate increases, we are close to having more people actually alive on earth than there is evidence of actually ever dying! If we discount disappearances, unconfirmed deaths, alien abductions, etc, a quick calculation will tell you that any one person's chance of actually dying in any one second of any one day is actually less than the chance of winning the national lottery (that is, if you have bought a national lottery ticket).

Think about it. At this very moment you are as likely to die as to win the national lottery.

You have to ask yourself, which would you prefer?

Also, notwithstanding the above, there is some evidence that death as we normally regard it, does not exist at all! Many religions and beliefs consider death as merely a prelude to an afterlife, a rebirth, a reincarnation or a resurrection.

If, however, you cannot accept any of these formulations, then you must believe that death is indeed inevitable, that nothing that ever mattered about you will still exist and that no-one will care.

You have to ask yourself, which would you prefer?

Q Is it possible to be a good person?

A I think I can put your mind at rest here. It is, in fact, NOT difficult to be a good person. Comparatively simple everyday tasks will help you attain this. Smile at the newsagent who serves you with your daily newspaper, clear your dog turds from your walk in the park. Actually listen when your partner tells you what they have bought at the supermarket.

Alternatively, you may wish to despise those who are less clever, less clean, less wealthy than yourself and spend every waking moment in pursuit of the edge that will give you superiority over others.

You may not be loved but you will be envied and admired which will feel much the same. You will learn to assuage any feelings of guilt or remorse and live contented after a fashion but always wary of others who seek the same as yourself.

You have to ask yourself, which would you prefer?

⧗

Q Is there such a thing as true love?

A I think I can put your mind at rest here. Not only is there such a thing as true love but it also quite easy to attain. Simply choose the object of your affection and treat them with absolute and unconditional devotion whether or not it is reciprocated. Continue to do so until, inevitably, you will be betrayed.

Choose to love, but always remember that grief is the ultimate consequence of love and it is the final gift you will be given.

Or choose not to love and eschew the pursuit of true love in favour of other, more selfish, concerns until your heart grows plump and hard and what remains of your shallow reflection fades in the cold stone mirror of life.

You have to ask yourself, which would you prefer?

Q What is the meaning of life?

A I think I can put your mind at rest here. For the very fact that you have asked this question suggests that you already know the answer. The meaning of life is that we are put on this earth to continually search for the meaning of life. We can either accept this or we have to presume that each living day is as unimportant as the day that precedes or follows it. That each thought is as worthless as any other. That each moment alive is no better or worse than each eternity dead.

You have to ask yourself, which would you prefer?

THE STONE MIRROR

Even the most willing pupil
cannot be taught not to see the stars

The eldest son of I, the Excellent Archer, had heard whispers that somewhere, on a lower sphere, lived mortals, who could be born, and suffer and die (words that had little meaning to the first son of a celestial master).

In the heavenly palace that was his home there was a hall called the Hall of the Three Footpaths. From each direction in the hall, apart from one, was a path that led, so he was told, to other forking paths that would eventually lead to anywhere on the celestial sphere (which was infinite). In the fourth direction, however, there was merely a large mirror, so large that it took up all of the wall and merged seamlessly into all its corners.

One day, The eldest son of I, the Excellent Archer, found himself staring into this mirror, and as he gazed more deeply he saw that the mirror, which was made of the finest polished bluestone, was not flat at all, but made up of hundreds of little figures, each carved in the form of a person. For the first time, also, he noticed that in front of the mirror, on the floor, was a handle, like that used to crush corn in gourds, or draw water from a canal.

Flushed with curiosity, he was tempted to turn this handle, and, since a son of a celestial god had never been taught how to contain temptation, he did. And, as soon as he touched the handle he imagined he saw little figures appear as shadows in the glossy smoothness of the mirror. And as he turned the handle. he began to realise that it turned finely carved ratchets in the stone mirror (which, despite its initial appearance, was not flat and featureless at all) and as he did so, it caused the little figures in the mirror to move mechanically in endless repetition, bending to scythe grass, or bowing in obsequience to the Emperor.

I, the Excellent Archer (who had shot nine suns from the sky to land as ravens on the earth and was omniscient and knew all his son's thoughts and actions) said to him, 'You have now seen some of the mortal world, which is a reflection of our own, as, indeed, we are reflections of it. That is why the stone mirror has been invisible you for so long. But now that you have discovered it, it cannot be hidden from you any longer. Now, what do you wish me to tell you?'

'Father,' he said, 'I would like you to tell me about all of the world below.' But then he reflected, for he was an intelligent boy. 'However, you have also taught me that words are infinite and meaning is ever shifting, and that not all that can be known can be fully expressed, even by the finest teacher. Therefore, I beg you, father, let me go there myself, so that I can learn to be mortal, and discover the meaning of life and death.'

I, the Excellent Archer, thought carefully about his son's request.

'Indeed, I have taught you that words are endless and their meaning elusive, and that even the careless words of foolish men can echo endlessly through the space of the spheres until they mean a hundred different things at once . However, the opposite can also be true and, indeed, a single word can, sometimes, mean more than it was discovered for, and it can even, for a short time, signify the whole universe. Scholars on earth have spent centuries juggling letters in combinations in order to discover the word that signifies a god.

'If I let you venture to earth as a mortal man, you must find a word that has a meaning more than simple letters or sounds can signify. It will be like fishing for a very small fish through a very small hole in the ice. You must remain until you discover it. Until you do so, you will not be able to return here.'

The son nodded his obedience, for he was now filled with a lust for the world that could not be signified in words.

'Your name in the mortal world,' said I, the Excellent Archer, 'will be Chiang Yee. It means the Silent Traveller. Travel in silence and in peace, my son.' And I, the Excellent Archer put his large bow-fingered hand over his son's tiny white hand and turned the handle again in the opposite direction. The tiny figures continued to move, but as they did so, the stone wheels found another gear and the mirror began to split and open like a gate. Behind it was a sky of the brightest blue imaginable—like nothing he had ever seen in his life. And that is how Chiang Yee, the eldest son of I, the Excellent Archer, came to earth as a mortal man.

THE LANGUAGE OF FLOWERS

Tender to your love as you would fry a small fish

On earth, Chiang Yee was adopted by Chiang Li, scribe to the Emperor's Censor.

His earthly father said to Chiang Yee, 'You are my son but not my son. I have been instructed by the imperial gods to nurture you and you will be nurtured well, but you will not sleep in my home. I have constructed a pagoda for you in my garden.

Chiang Li had one daughter, Chen Li, and she was regarded by the standards of the time, as very beautiful. She wore by day a red robe dyed with essence of a shellfish and with little sewn white rosettes down the side. She taught Chiang Yee the language of flowers. They would walk together each day among the scented gardens with their tiers of rocks and small trees, and by the river where she would pick a blossom. 'Each of these has a meaning that is peculiar to itself,' she said. 'They mean little on their own, but if you were to tie them in a bouquet they would form a story.

Then you may send them to your loved one.'

Chiang Yee was entranced by Chen Li, the way she walked and spoke and her easy acquaintance with the language of flowers. He enquired how she had learned so much.

'I am very clever,' she said, 'I can paint with a sable brush, inscribe with a split stem and tie a silk ribbon with chopsticks.'

THE EMINENT PROFESSORS

Does the child who learns to count know his days are numbered

So Chiang Yee lived in the garden of the scribe to the Emperor's censor and he was happy enough. Along with Chen Li he was attended upon by tutors and he was taught to make birds out of paper, to throw a pot on a wheel, to carve chopsticks, to inscribe on a clay tablet, to paint on parchment and to count on an abacus.

After a little time, however, a time in which Chiang Yee had excelled at all of his subjects, his earthly father came to him and told him it was now time for him to proceed to the most important of his classes, the class in grammar. So Chiang Yee was introduced to a tall man who identified himself as the Grammarian and who took him to a little room brightly lit by lanterns in all four corners that was set apart from the other classrooms.

In the room was a kind of cradle, with paper straps at its corners. Chiang Yee was placed in the cradle by the Grammarian and his hands tied by the paper straps. Then his legs were lifted upwards and apart and tied also. When his robes were raised his taut buttocks and white thighs were completely exposed. The Grammarian indicated a rack on the wall ahead of him. On it was a series of bamboo canes of decreasing thickness. 'These are our most eminent professors,' he said, 'and they are here to instruct you.'

And then the master took the thickest of the professors from the rack and administered it to Chiang Yee on the tender parts of his little mortal body and Chiang Yee roared and roared until, thankfully, after some time, the lesson was concluded.

This form of instruction continued daily with the master choosing, in succession, the thinner of the rods from the rack. And each day the sensation grew more severe and Chiang Yee retreated to his cot to rest his roasted and splintered buttocks in a soothing balm of iced water. The Grammarian took great pride in his work in this respect. 'It takes many years to master the application of the professors,' he said, 'the most eminent masters can apply the finest of the professors to a bean curd without breaking its surface.'

Then, one day, Chiang Yee said, 'Master, you have spoken often of the eminent professors and the skill that must be acquired in their use. Yet not once have you allowed me to use one of them. I am always tied in the cradle and the professors minister to me. Why cannot I use the professors myself?'

The Grammarian shook his head. 'It is because you do not understand the answer to that question that you cannot yet graduate. However, now that you have chosen to ask me so, tonight will be your last lesson and it will continue until you understand.'

So that evening Chiang Yee returned to the little room and was surprised to see that his earthly father and Chen Li were also there. He started as if to speak, but the Grammarian raised his hand to silence him. 'Remove your robe,' he said. Chiang Yee blushed to think that Chen Li would see his naked thighs and buttocks but he acquiesced to his master.

Once again Chiang Yee was placed in the cradle, but he was now so moulded to its contours that he fitted it with comfort and there was no need for the paper ties. 'It is now time for you to graduate,' said the Grammarian. 'You may ask one question before the conferment.'

'Chiang Yee asked, 'why are we not alone as usual for this lesson?'

'We are alone,' the Grammarian said, 'or rather, *you* are alone.'

The Grammarian then reached down and took something from the bottom row of the rack. 'This is our most eminent professor'. Chiang Yee looked and looked, but he could see nothing at all in the hand of the Grammarian. However, as the Grammarian moved his arm he thought he could hear a low swish, like a slight breeze through blades of grass. 'So far', said the Grammarian, your lessons in this class have been rudimentary. Tonight they will last until time itself stops and then they will be complete.' And then the Grammarian applied the professor, or the professor applied the Grammarian, for, as it happened, they were one and the same. And, as the professor swung rhymically, Chiang Yee saw the Grammarian's hand also disappear, then his arm, until there was nothing but the rhythm of the sensations in Chiang Yee himself. And time stopped, and the sensations that Chiang Yee felt were exquisite and unbearable. He did not weep tears, but he understood, before the graduation was complete, that the art of employing the professor was not of itself significant, and that to suffer the professor's sting was to become the professor, and that was where knowledge began.

THE DWARF GUIDE

Live your life as you would peel your only grape

Chiang Yee longed to speak with Chen Li and to understand the language of the flowers as well as she. But his earthly father told him that Chen Li had also graduated with distinction and, thus, as a reward, she was to become concubine to the monks in the mountain fortress to the north. 'First, however, she will have her eyes removed, so she can not cast envious glances at the mere materials of the world, and her tongue removed, so that she cannot utter words of deception or rebellion. The monks prefer it that way'. He shrugged.

'It is also time for you to depart, my half son. The gods have determined that you should be sent to the Imperial City to learn to be a scribe there.'

So Chiang Yee packed a little sack with some stones and waxed flowers that Chen Li had given to him and a little clay tablet to record his adventures.

While he was so doing a very small man came to attend on him. 'I am to be your guide,' he said, 'you cannot find your way to the palace on your own.'

So Chiang Yee prepared to set off, but the dwarf showed no inclination to move. 'You do not expect me to walk!' he stated indignantly. 'Do you not think it would take an eternity to reach the palace with my short legs.'

'Well, what will we do?' Asked Chiang Yee.

'Take me on your shoulders,' he said. 'That way I will be able to see far ahead and spot any trouble.'

So Chiang Yee took the dwarf on his shoulders and set off. It went well enough until they came to a ford at a river. As they crossed the water, Chiang Yee's legs buckled and his feet sank into the silt. He didn't feel he could go any further and he stretched up to remove the dwarf from his shoulders. The little man helped. 'Help! Do you want me to drown?'

'I can't hold you anymore, you're too heavy!'

'Of course I am! Don't you know that dwarfs grow heavier over water. The longer you take the harder it will be to reach the other side.'

Chiang Yee reflected. Was it not the lesson of his masters that what would not be endured must be endured? So he continued and didn't relent until they had bridged the other side and then he released the dwarf to rest.

'No, we cannot stop here,' said the dwarf.

'Why not,' asked Chiang Yee, 'when my legs are rested we will travel further and faster. Perhaps we should camp here for the night.'

The dwarf sniffed all around the ground. 'No,' he said, 'we will move on.'

'But why?' said Chiang Yee, 'Is there something unpleasant here?'

'You really know nothing about dwarves,' the dwarf said. 'Dwarves can smell the future. Dwarves are like little gods, you know.'

The dwarf shook his head and made a strange sound. 'There is a change in circumstances. There is danger ahead, the enemies of the Emperor are in possession of some of the Emperor's land. It will not last long.' He added, 'the Emperor will grant them his mercy and destroy them when he feels fit.'

'Who are these enemies of the Emperor?'

'Barbarians. They fly across the steppes on horses that are fiercer than bears or dragons. They wear waistbands of bamboo and ivory sheaths around their man parts. They are bred from crocodiles. You wouldn't want to meet a barbarian.'

Chiang Yee thought it better to agree. So, at the dwarf's insistence, they travelled to a nearby village. 'Your father has some influence here,' he said. 'We will find you a position and then I will leave. I have really done quite enough for a mere dwarf.'

THE FOUNDRY MASTER

If in the morning the sky is uninteresting,
the shepherd's day is done

In the village, it was decided that Chiang Yee, to keep him occupied, would be apprenticed for a while to a Foundry Master.

The days passed by and Chiang Yee learned much. The Foundry Master pointed to strange lights glowing in many colours in the skies by night. They are portents he said, of some great change.

The foundry made swords and spears for the emperor's army, but the days grew colder and the army still did not come. Coal still arrived in carts and the Foundry Master toiled by the day and then drank tea and slept. Chiang Yee lay on a couch by the fire and watched the Foundry Master sleep.

The Foundry Master had one and one half legs. The bottom half of the left was replaced by a wooden peg. 'When I was much younger I fell in the fire,' he said. 'Beware of fire, it is both beautiful and dangerous.'

Chiang Yee was a good servant to the Foundry Master who grew fond of the boy, so in his waking hours he would sometimes tell stories to Chiang Yee and one of the stories that he told him was of the invention of the colour red.

THE INVENTION OF THE COLOUR RED

The rainbow only sees in black and white

The country in which Chiang Hong was fortunate enough to be born was rigorous in its governance and intolerant of its own inadequacies, but there was poetry and compassion and some men were happy there.

Nevertheless, it was a country completely without colour. The certainties of black and white and the nuances of grey were in every way sufficient for its inhabitants to describe the world in all its complexity.

And then an extraordinary thing happened. Simultaneously, by the exigences of what has been called coincidence, two learned men who had never met: one a noted professor of philology who had translated epic ballads from tongues centuries old, the other a mathematician who had discovered equations to describe seashells and snowflakes, had the same thought.

Basically, the first of these learned men spent many hours studying the grass and the trees of the countryside; the other, similarly, studied the sky and the clouds. One decided that the grass and the trees were so beautiful and so particular that they needed what was later to be called a colour to describe them. From his study of languages and the meaning of words he conjured up a name for this description. He called it green.

The other, on staring into the sky on a notably cloudless day decided that it should be named after a particularly beautiful combination of letters. He called it blue.

These discoveries came as a revelation to the people. They were earnestly debated in the academy and the constitution of the land was rewritten to include the right to call by name the colours blue and green. Indeed, the discoverers of these by now established concepts were rewarded with the titles of the Master of the Colour Green and the Master of the Colour Blue. Each dawn thousands of men and women and children gathered for the sun to appear and reveal the colours of green and blue which met at the horizon and, between them, represented the whole of the classifiable world.

Chiang Hong followed this development with the fervour of all the converted. There was something peculiar about him. He had been a difficult child, who had never blindly obeyed the orders of his parents and teachers. Chiang Hong was stubborn and this contrariness often led him to question the edicts of even the highest authorities.

Therefore, it was no great surprise that one day Chiang Hong did not rise to see the colours pronounced by dawn, but instead waited until sunset and sat studying the horizon and the fields and the sky.

And at one moment, when the sun had almost but not

quite sunk beneath the horizon, Chiang Hong saw something extraordinary. Between the heavens and the earth there appeared a bright strip of sky that was not black, not white, neither blue nor green. Instantly Chiang Hong thought of a name for this new colour, he would name it after himself (he was also prone to vanity) and name it red.

Chiang Hong wandered the world seeking to name new appearances of the colour red. He found it in the solitary flowers that often appeared in fields of barley or corn, he found it in the cloaks of peasants dyed in an essence derived from shellfish, he found it in the bloodshot eyes of the drinkers in the tavern.

All these discoveries were reported in the streets and the inns and Chiang Hong became the subject of some celebrity. Some said that he should be named the Master of the Colour Red, but the Academy would not agree. A person of such humble origins as Chiang Hong, in their opinion, could not merit such an eminent title.

Nevertheless, as public interest accumulated and the Academy relented. It agreed that Chiang Hong should be allowed to address the Academy to present his new theory of the colour red. Thereafter he would be questioned by its most senior members including the Masters of the Colour Green and of the Colour Blue.

Chiang Hong had prepared his speech to the Academy but was surprised that when he opened his mouth to speak the company began to clap their hands, then make hooting sounds and whistles. He stopped and tried again but he was not allowed to say a single word. Then he felt a heavyness in his head and everything faded to something that was no colour at all.

When Chiang Hong awoke he found himself sitting in an upright chair. His hands were bound behind his back and his feet tied to the legs of the chair. A rope was taut around his neck.

When he realised what they were about to do there was a

moment when terror turns to pain in which he conceived an entirely new colour that he thought to name yellow.

But, as it turned out, the Masters of the Colours Green and Blue were right, and the burning coals were of the colours green and blue. Chiang Hong, with his sad black eyeless sockets could never name colours again although he imagined them, fiercely, for the rest of his waking and dreaming days, which were mercifully short.

THE PRECIPICE

Is the butterfly too beautiful to learn how to sin?

'Patience and forebearance,' the Foundry Master said, 'that is what we need. 'I don't know why the gods have chosen me to do this, but this is what I do, and I will serve the Emperor doing so until it is my time.'

He spoke to Chiang Yee as he stoked the coals. 'Life is short. We are all clinging to the edge of a precipice. When I feel that I serve no purpose any more, it will be time to let go.'

Chiang Yee served the Foundry Master and things remained the same for a little while until, with the rainy season approaching, the Emperor decided to withdraw his forces for a while. They passed by the village, some walking, some tied to the side of elephants.

Chiang Yee tried to get soldiers to take him with them to the emperor's palace where he had originally been meant to go but the soldiers were weary and wouldn't listen. 'If the Emperor has need of a boy,' one said, 'he will send for you.'

The barbarians followed the emperor's forces south, harrying and molesting them when they could. When they came upon the village, the Foundry Master, on his one and one half legs, couldn't run from them. They caught Chiang Yee and tied him by his throat to the trunk of a tree. They let him watch while they played with the Foundry Master and his forge and his fire until there was not much of any of them left. The Foundry Master, as it turned out, clung to the precipice of life much longer than he had intended to or wanted to.

THE BAMBOO CAGE

Accept each day's living as a lesson in dying

They did not kill Chiang Yee. Instead they took him back to their settlement. They put him in a bamboo cage on the ground near the place they kept their pigs. The cage was too small to allow him to stand or sit, and, in fact, he had to lie in the mud bent over double. They fed him on the same swill as the pigs. He was completely naked, and lay in his own dirt. Sometimes the children would torment him. The boys would burn his toes with hot coals and the girls tickled his member with a long feather to see it rise and fall.

One day a barbarian girl came to Chiang Yee in his bamboo cage—a girl of about Chiang Yee's own age or a little older. She was naked except for paint that covered her body and ended with a striped face. Surprisingly, she spoke to Chiang Yes in his own language.

'They torment you every day', she said, 'and yet you do not cry.'

Chiang Yee was surprised. 'Why do you speak to me?' he asked, 'and how do you know the Emperor's language?'

'I was captured too', she said. She turned her back to him. It was crossed with deep scars.

'They gave me these,' she said, 'and then they decided to make me into an animal. And I have been so since.' Then she undid the cords that fastened the bamboo cage and entered it, squeezing close to his body.

Chiang Yee thought that she may have wished to speak to him further, but she did not. She did something that for a moment made him into an animal too. And Chiang Yee was uncertain for some time if she was indeed a girl or a creature. And then she left him to writhe in pain and when the children returned they mocked him and tormented him more than ever.

Chiang Yee endured this for half of one year, until the rains to the south were depleted and the valley was once again clear for the Emperor's forces to raid the village with many additional men and scotch the rebellion. They enjoyed the women one by one, and they did not allow the men to die like warriors, as they were not regarded as subjects of the Empire.

THE CUTTY STOOL

The slowest snail may still be in a hurry

The Emperor's men taught Chiang Yee to walk again and agreed to keep him with them until they returned south. One day they were camped near a river adjacent to a small town and Chiang Yee took some time to wander around. He saw men heading to market with furs hanging from yokes around their necks, He saw old women sewing shoes. He saw girls wading in the river feeling for jade with their toes and this aroused some desire in him that he did not understand

After a while he came to a market square where he saw a crowd gathered around. In the centre of the square was a boy selling trinkets.

'These are the symbols of the goddess of love, the most beautiful thing you will ever see', said the boy. 'Now I will show you what they will enable you to do'.

Then the boy sat down on a small three-legged stool he had carried, and as he did so he dropped his trousers from round his slender waist. He grabbed the stool with both his hands and closed his eyes. Almost immediately his little brown organ began to rise until it was full and erect. Then, within only a little while, alone and without any helping hand, it had risen to its full proportion and, before the whole congregation, spent its seed.

The crowd applauded and cheered with many a lewd aside and coarse laughter and the boy sold many of his little trinkets.

When all had been done, Chiang Yee did not leave with the others but instead followed the boy into the shade of some trees where he was counting his coins.

'Please excuse me', he said, 'but I need to know more about the powers of the love goddess.'

The boy looked at him 'If you have some coins…'

Chiang Yee shook his head. 'I have no coins, but perhaps I can ask my dwarf. He may have some.'

The boy laughed. 'You give your coins to your dwarf! You are a fool!' But then he smiled and said 'It is only a trick. Look!'

The boy presented the stool to Chiang Yee for examination. Chiang Yee realised that it was not quite as it had first seemed. In the bottom of the stool was a bore hole and suspended by a string from the bottom of the stool was a peg of sorts, split and round and slightly bent at the top, that could be fitted through the hole.

'While holding on to the stool, I apply it to the rear orifice and it causes the effect. Try it.'

So Chiang Yee divested himslf of his robes and sat on the stool and, clumslly, applied the peg through the bore hole, which caused him to gasp with surprise. But his organ did not rise as had the organ of the brash boy. He applied the peg again with more vigour but with no immediate effect. The boy was looking on with an expression that Chiang Yee could not name but he suspected that there was some laughter around the lines of his face.

Chiang Yee had a premonition of failure and tried harder,

shifting the peg into several positions that may have proved efficacious, causing him to winch a little.

He averted his eyes to avoid the gaze of the boy, but he still imagined him eyeing his futile attempts and felt, for the first time, shame at his own impotence and inadequacy,

With this feeling, he began to blush, and as he blushed, his organ began to rise, until it was thin and pointed and red-tipped.

And yet Chiang Yee, who had never spent before, did not know how he could finish the deed to satisfaction. So he began to think. He thought of all the things he had seen since he had come to earth. He thought of Chen Li and the language of flowers, of the magical lights in the sky, of the cradle in the academy and the administrations of the professors.

Then he thought of the monks in the mountains and of Chen Li and of her pitiable little body with its bandaged eyes and vacant mouth. And he did feel pity, but he was not sure whether it was for poor Chen Li or for Chiang Yee himself.

And then it came, like a spurt of molten bronze from the foundry, and Chiang Yee spent.

And it was hotter than any possible passion that he could have imagined.

THE TREE

The oldest tree stump holds a memory of
singing birds and falling leaves

The soldiers eventually approached their barracks. They told Chiang Yee that the imperial palace was no more than two days walk away and they set him on his way with some basic provisions.

After a while he came upon a man sitting cross-legged beneath a tall tree that stood alone in a patch of brown ground. The man seemed distracted and was swaying slowly back and forth. Out of curiosity, Chiang Yee approached him.

'What are you doing,' he asked.

The man did not turn around but did not seemed surprised to hear his voice.

'Oh, I am the imperial poet and the Emperor has instructed me to write a poem that is a tree.'

'Have you done so?'

The Emperor's poet showed Chiang Yee a parchment he held in his hand:

You
thought
that I would die
as men will do
but here still am I
transfigured as a tree

First thoughts of root and trunk
froze leaf and flower fruit
but then my tree-like qualities
emerged
I have settled into my frills and boughs.
When I was a man
I could make you mock
or lust or cry
But now my poetry is of a different sort
under my arbours gather
in the slow creaking wind
I will make you
sigh

'It looks very like a tree to me,' said Chiang Yee.

The poet shrugged. 'Perhaps, but time will tell. The tree will become the poem, or the poem will become the tree—or perhaps I will become the tree; the art of poetry cannot be hurried. The

Emperor's allocated span is seven years to write a poem.'

Chiang Yee continued a little further until he came upon a bank of sand by the bow of a river. A man was drawing a shape in the sand with a stick.

'What have you drawn?' asked Chiang Yee.

'The Emperor has given me the task of making a drawing that is a bird. I have thought about it for seven years, and now I have completed my task.'

Chiang Yee looked at the shape in the sand. It was a fine drawing indeed of a bird, but as he viewed it, some water sweeping round the bend of the river seeped into the strand and the shape began to disappear. The Emperor's artist was not distracted and did not take his eyes of his work until it was completely gone.

THE HANGING MAN

Not only the blind can fish in muddy waters

As Chiang Yee approached the city walls, he came across a strange scene. A man was stretched by his tied arms between two stakes. His face was bound in silk with only his eyes exposed which moved steadily from side to side. Behind him some men were building what looked like a trestle. To the side a little clot of men, women and children were arguing with three men clothed in black

A little further off, another man, in what Chiang Yee took to be imperial robes, was examining a scroll.

'Excuse me', Chiang Yee said, 'could you tell me what is happening here?'

The man ceased examining the scroll. 'Do you have any business in these parts?' he asked.

'Yes I have', said Chiang Yee. 'I have been called to the Emperor's court.' He added 'To be trained as a scribe.'

'Hmm,' the man intoned sonorously. 'Well, as a scribe you may have to record mercies such as these.'

'Mercies?'

'Yes, this man has been chosen to succumb to the Emperor's mercy. He is sentenced to be suspended by the head between two planks.'

'He is to be executed, then?'

The man gave Chiang Yee a strange look. 'He is sentenced to be suspended by the head between two planks. That is all. If it were an execution, his head would be severed with an axe.'

'Will he not die, then?'

'I suspect that is likely, but that is the choice of the gods.'

'What has he done?' I asked.

'He is accused of violating a child and causing its death by intimate penetration.'

Chiang Yee thought about this. 'Who are those people?' he asked, 'and why are they shouting?'

'They are his family,' the man replied. 'They have come with evidence that another has confessed to the same offence in the next city and has been executed for it.'

'Should the man not be released then, if he is not guilty?'

He shook his head. 'Are you a poet?' He asked. 'There are too many of your sort about. You had better change your tune if you are to fit in here.'

'But, if another committed the crime, surely the man is not guilty of it!'

'That is a very strange idea. Just because someone is guilty of an offence in another province why should that have any effect on the Emperor's justice here?'

'But it is the same crime, it cannot have been committed by two people!'

'You poets,' the man exclaimed. 'You live in the temporal world of story. In the world of jurisprudence, it is entirely acceptable that this man is guilty of the offence here and another man is guilty of the offence elsewhere. It is quite logical.'

'It doesn't seem fair!' Chiang Yee exclaimed.

'Fair', he said, and chewed the word around in his mouth a little as if it were an exotic fruit.

He waved Chiang Yee away. 'Personally, I don't think you have the correct demeanour to serve in the Imperial City. Do you think you are a god, that you can judge this man? Luckily, the Emperor is merciful and pray that you may be subject to his mercy also.'

THE IMPERIAL CITY

The city will still retain the village in its heart

Chiang Yee headed towards the gates of the city and tried not to look back. He heard a sort of wailing and a swishing sound but he neither looked over his shoulder or diminished his stride.

As he got closer to where he presumed the city to be he expected it to appear before him, but there was nothing, only a haze that obliterated the horizon between the the land and the sky. Suddenly he felt lost. Then he spied a small figure squatting on the ground ahead. It was the dwarf guide.

'Ah,' he said, 'so you have found your way at last!'

Chiang Yee considered. 'I have come here, and I have had many adventures on the way.'

'Adventures?' said the dwarf. 'What do I know about adventures, I am merely a dwarf!'

It occurred to Chiang Yee that the dwarf might be able to help him find the Imperial City. 'If you're still my guide,' he said, then show me where the Imperial City is.'

'Do you know the name of the city?' asked the dwarf.

'No,' said Chiang Yee, I just know it is the Imperial City.'

'The city must not be confused with the words that describe

it,' said the dwarf, 'but in order to see the city you must know its name. The city has been rebuilt many times and has been given many names. Once it was Consternation, then Confidence, then Constancy, and once it was Inferiority, then Ire, then Uncartainty.'

'What is it called now?'

'How should I know? I'm a dwarf. Think hard and it may be called the name you wish.'

Chiang Yee thought hard and after a little while a name popped into his head and then the city did appear, its walls forming through the shimmering mist.

Chiang Yee was heartened and hastened towards the city.

'You too must have a name,' the dwarf called after him, 'but once you are within, of course, you will be given another one and you must lose the memory of any other name.'

THE EMPEROR'S LIBRARY

The unread book cannot be unwritten

As Chiang Yee approached the city he was surprised to see that it took various forms. The walls themselves seemed variously gold, or silver, and sometimes like mountains or clouds.

However, when he came upon them, he saw that the walls of the city were made of lacquered tiles that shone with a bright translucence (he was later told that they extended for six walking days and were washed down with rosewater every day).

At the entrance were five armed guards, their polished pointed helmets mirroring the spears they held upright.

'Halt, what is your business?' asked one guard.

Chiang Yee told them that he had been sent to be a scribe to the Emperor. The guards debated for some time among themselves, then one said, 'Come, I will take you to the Assistant Librarian.'

The library was a grand place with balconies of shelves each containing rolls of parchments. Sections were divided by screens of zitan wood, and censers burned aromatically in every corner.

The Assistant Librarian was a portly man dressed in a long white robe. His hair was spare and his eyes were not eyes. They were like two large yolkless eggs. It was evident that he was completely blind. He ran his fingers over the head and face of Chiang Yee.

'I see,' he said. 'You are here to be a scribe to the Emperor. I am the Assistant Librarian. While you are here you will answer to the name I will give you and that will be Chiang Yee.'

Chiang Yee was pleasantly surprised that his name would remain Chiang Yee. He remembered that it meant The Silent Traveller and he silently cursed himself for his curiosity that bade him open his mouth far more enough than he thought he should. He determined that in the imperial palace, his duty would be to observe, rather than to speak.

The Assistant Librarian showed him a table in the centre of the library. There were betel boxes in the shape of geese in each corner filled with quills and in the centre was a large pot of black ink, its surface smooth and shiny. 'The inkpot contains all the conceivable and inconceivable books in the world', said the Assistant Librarian. 'Thus the library is infinite, and, as you know, our word for infinity is the same as our word for chaos'.

The Assistant Librarian set Chiang Yee the task of inscribing the names of all the Emperor's courtiers. According to their position and their vitality, their names would be inscribed in either gold, vermilion or black.

'This is a simple enough but essential task,' he said, 'if you do well, who knows, you may be rewarded with another post, perhaps servant to the Emperor's censor.'

So Chiang Yee laboured away at his task. He seldom rested, and always with his eyes open, so nothing much in the world escaped Chiang Yee. Apart from the liitle time he spent in his bedchamber, he dedicated his time to the inscriptions, although he noticed that, over time, many more of the courtiers' names were inscribed in black denoting their passing to another realm of existence.

Chiang Yee was, nevertheless, always curious, and one day he couldn't hold his tongue and he said to the Assistant Librarian. 'I know that you are the Assistant Librarian and a very eminent and important person indeed, but I wondered where is the Librarian and if I ever will see him.'

'Hmm,' the Assistant Libarrian replied, 'that may be possible, but it is unlikely. Hereabouts the Librarian is akin to a god. Personally, I have never encountered him.'

After some time, the Assistant Librarian called Chiang Yee to him. 'You are a prodigy, and the Emperor is pleased with you. It is now the emperor's pleasure to make you an imperial servant of the emperor's inventory!'

Chiang Yee thought that this must be a much grander job than that of servant to the Emperor's censor so he was eager to discover what it involved.

The Assistant Librarian showed him a list.

'This was composed by one of the emperor's finest listers, a man of great philosophy and demeanour but intemperate habits. Lists are very important to the Emperor. This is a list of the Emperor's animals.'

1. Belonging to the Emperor
2. Embalmed
3. Tame
4. Suckling Pigs
5. Sirens
6. Stray dogs
7. Included in the present classification
8. Frenzied

9. Innumerable
10. Drawn with a very fine camel hair
11. Et cetera
12. Having just broken the Emperor's water pitch
13. That from a long way off look like flies

Chiang Yee looked at the list. 'It seems a very fine list, indeed,' he said, but how was it constructed.'

'Ah,' said the Assistant Librarian, 'what you must understand is that the learning of listing is in the making of lists, and that is where you must begin.'

He added, 'There are some principles, however. The Emperor's Chief Lister has made a list of types of lists. There are various categories: chaotic enumerations, ineffable mirabilia... You will soon see.'

Will I ever get to meet the Emperor's Chief Lister,' asked Chiang Yee.

'Personally,' replied The Assistant Librarian, 'I have never encountered him.'

THE EMPEROR

The one-eyed man may see the most

Chiang Yee laboured away making lists and lists of lists. From the courtiers that passed through the library he learned more about the Emperor and the Emperor's palace. He learned that below the Emperor's bedchamber lay a replica of the world, the trees carved out of jade and the rivers comprised from flowing mercury. He learned that the Emperor had a very particular nose. For his pleasure, concubines should be born smelling of the yellow jujube flower. Their eyelashes and eyebrows should be lacquered with gold and their robes laced with velvety wild flower: lotuses, water lilies and peonies (this made Chiang Yee remember the flower language of Chen Li). Their ornaments were made of gilt lapis, cat's eye, turquoise and moonstone. Their breath was savoured with an extract made from swallow's nests. This was unusual, but the Emperor liked it that way.

The more eminent of the courtiers wore summer robes of yellow silk laced with pearls and winter robes of crimson silk lined with white fox fur. They drank wine from jade bowls inscribed with dragons and the words of fine poetry. It was rumoured that the finest wine from the finest jade bowls was blessed with a powder that bestowed immortality. Chiang Yee wondered if ever he could aspire to become one of the Emperor's eminent courtiers.

He continued to work at his listing. However, one day, to Chiang Yee's astonishment, the Assistant Librarian came to him and said. 'You have laboured hard and well. It is time for you to be granted an audience with the Emperor.'

The Assistant Librarian, escorted by two courtiers, led him to the Emperor's inner chamber.

On the couch in the centre of the chamber lay the body of a small frail man with wires for a beard. His body was a criss-cross shaped from bones under a silk sheet. The skin of his face was tough and leathery and wrinkled and white. His eyelids were stitched together with the blackened holes of rotting threads. The lips of his mouth were cleaved together with thorn needles.

The Assistant Librarian explained that soon the Emperor would soon be riding the stork to become the master of celestial masters.

Chiang Yee had descended to the mortal earth to discover death, yet still he did not understand it. 'Surely the Emperor is already dead, as he does not breath and his heart does not beat. Are not those the signifiers of life.'

The Assistant Librarian sighed. 'You have seen so much and have learned so little'. He pointed to several small caskets and bottles on a shelf nearby. 'The organs of the Emperor have been removed for preparation for his journey. He took a small jar from the shelf. 'See, the eyes are preserved in vitriol to protect them from the sun. We minister to the Emperor with the same care required for his absolution whether he is whole or incomplete.'

THE LABYRINTH

He who sleeps with both eyes open may still not see

When Chiang Yee and the Assistant Librarian left the Emperor's bedchamber the palace was altogether different. The walls were darker and strange shadows seemed to run through them. Chiang Yee did not know whether the Assistant Librarian could see these changes but he did notice that he seemed somehow startled.

Then Chiang Yee heard in the distance the tolling of a bell, insistent and continuous.

'What does the tolling of the bell mean?' he asked the Assistant Librarian?'

The Assistant Librarian hesitated. 'I am just an Assistant Librarian, therefore I do not necessarily know what everything means.' He thought for a moment. 'I know that the tolling of the bell means change, but it could mean more than one form of change. However, it is recorded in the protocols of the palace that, in order to protect the Emperor from change, the palace will, when the bell tolls, become a labyrinth.' Then he added, 'But a labyrinth not like any normal labyrinth: a labyrinth that has a different solution for each one who enters it. That way only the more astute of the emperor's courtiers will be able to enter and leave the palace. It will protect him from the coming of the Demon God.'

For some reason, Chiang Yee was alarmed to hear this. 'What is the Demon God?' he asked.

'The Demon God, it is said, will come to earth in the guise of a man, but on his body will be inscribed a secret word that, spoken aloud, will have the power to destroy even the Emperor. The Demon God will be exactly in the form of a man, but he will not be able to sleep or laugh or cry.'

Chiang Yee thought of this and suddenly he felt a sensation he was not familiar with: fear.

He turned to the Assistant Librarian. 'What would make a man who is not a man become a man?'

'Suffering until death.'

'And what if he shall not die?'

'All will die when they have suffered enough.'

And then the Assistant Librarian looked with his blind eyes directly into Chiang Yee's eyes and he began to quiver and shake and then a dark shadow seemed to reach out from the walls and began to engulf him. Then he shrunk and shrivelled until there was nothing left of him at all.

THE ASCENSION

The pendulous weight knows it has yet to fall

Chiang Yee ran through the labyrinth to escape from the shadow that had consumed the Assistant Librarian. He had no sense of which direction he was heading but suddenly, he stumbled and realised he was in his own bedchamber.

In a frenzy he tore off his clothes. His chamber, by now, had grown to contain many mirrors of all shapes and sizes. He believed that these were all-powerful and all-revealing. Although the world of the library was both infinite and chaotic, he thought, in comparison his own body was limited and absolute. He calmed himself and, by process of elimination, using the different mirrors, he inspected every part of his own body, even the soles of his feet and his gums and lips, his shaven head and the interiors of all the orifices. Eventually, when he was satisfied that no part of his body was contaminated with the sign of the Demon God, he paused and, at that moment, the bell stopped tolling.

He didn't know that the symbols of godhood were concealed in the creases of his eyelids and that was why he was forbidden to sleep or to cry.

THE WORD

The largest fish may yet be found in the smallest lake

Chiang Yee ran through corridor after corridor until at last he came to a door. Beyond the door he passed into an open field and behind him the Emperor's palace dissolved into air.

A tiny wind blew through the grass. Elsewhere all was silent. In front of him stood, in receding ranks for miles around, the Emperor's warriors. They were an inhuman army, each shaped in clay, immobile, one after one, in tiers and ranks.

There Chiang Yee stood, the solitary figure in this frozen landscape. A small naked man or not-man.

And then Chiang Yee realised. He had recorded many words on his travels and he thought that perhaps the word he sought was love, or pain, or death. But one word contained all those words, and many others. It was a word that only man could utter. Chiang Yee longed for the flower speak of Chen Li, for the instruction of the eminent professors, for the violated child who had tormented him. He longed to see the Assistant Librarian again or the Emperor's poet and artist and censor and even the dwarf guide. But there was no-one now but himself.

At last Chiang Yee wept, long hot tears that welled and overflowed and dripped and filled the water pitcher with a human rain.

And the Rain Dragon saw his tears and, taking pity on the earth, showered it in his fertilising rain. And then the Emperor's army, like all the Emperor's wealth, melted to nothingness in the flow. And Chiang Yee shouted the word that meant the universe, and it reverberated around the terracotta ears of the Emperor's army. And that word was ALONE.

THE STONE MIRROR

The sword that believes it is a ploughshare is still a sword

Chiang Yee opened his eyes and saw the receding blue sky. In one hand, now, was the handle that turned the stone mirror. His other hand was contained within the large bow-fingered hand of I, the Excellent Archer. Slowly, he turned the handle and gradually the stone mirror closed and once again became whole. And the little figures mechanically, in endless repetition, bowed in contrition to the Emperor, and the warriors lifted their bows and shields, and the professors thrashed their pupils with bamboo canes, and the monks copulated with their concubines, in a steady rhythm. And all was right again with the conceivable world.

BABYLON

Charmaine found the slight dusky stranger in a coffee house down by the boardwalk. It was a hot night after the Mardi Gras. Fireflies tumbled through the humid air and the fragile dark sky hung above the river ready to crack with thunder.

Charmaine was slim and brown like chocolate, dressed in black with little red rosettes on her stockings. She realised that the stranger, who called himself Georgy, was not only frail for a young man but weak-eyed. He said he came from somewhere very far to the south. He was in New Orleans on business. He said he collected books and wrote poems and stories. He said he had happened into the little courtyard coffee house by chance whilst wandering the streets as the heat wouldn't let him sleep in his hotel bed.

'Yo looking for business?' Charmaine had asked, but she soon realised that the young man didn't know what she meant.

'Ain everybody knows what go on in here,' she had said, 'but in the Quarter nobody much gonna huckle yo. Yo take care though.'

Georgy said that he was careful. 'I like New Orleans', he said, 'it reminds me of my own decadent colonial city and of Rimbaud and Baudelaire.

'Yo sure is strange' she said.

'I'm sorry', he said, 'I've been to the golden city of Edinburgh, and the two Cordobas and the labyrinth of London but most of my time I spend in my library with my books.'

'Well, N'Awlins is pretty good town', Charmaine admitted, 'but since the depression there ain so much here to do. That Huey Long, now, he the main man, but he ain gonna do nothing for the negro. Yo gotta look out for yourself.'

'And how do you do that', asked Georgy.

Charmaine laughed. She took her little, slim-fingered hand with its long fingernails and gently touched him on the cheek.

'Honey, you don know… '

She turned away to the side of the courtyard where some flowers were growing on a trellis. She twined a few limp green tendrils in her fingers. The courtyard was empty and there was no business for her that night.

'Hey,' she called to Georgy, 'yo like stories. We got plenty stories here in N'Awlins.' She told him about Marie Laveau, the Voodoo queen, of Madame Marie Lalaurie who tortured her negro slaves in her house in the Quarter until one day it burnt down and she was never seen again.

Georgy was interested. 'History is an accumulation of a series of coincidences', he said, but the writer of fiction can exhaust all the possibilities of history and create even more'. He told her a strange story about a country where everything that happened was determined by the drawing of lots.

'Spose it's like a crap game', she said, 'yo jus don know when yo turn is up.'

She picked a rose from the garden trellis, a little scarlet bloom distilled from a hundred years in the wormwood swamp of Louisiana.

'Here yo are', she said, 'Spare a dollar for a pore nigra girl. My pot's done empty tonight.'

Georgy gave her a five dollarbill for the rose. He said he would write a poem for it before he returned home.

'I knows a pome', she said. 'My mamma got it from her mamma.'

Charmaine leaned her back against the iron grille and recited the poem in a strained but melodic English:

There's many mile to Babylon,
Four score an tin,

The cat will crack, the cock will crow,
The rose will grow agin.

The words reverberated a little in the evening air. The evening grew hot and limp after the storm had broken and the old waters of the Mississippi ran so sluggish that even the mudfish had nothing much to do. Then New Orleans settled itself to wait for the dawn and a cooler day and for the New Deal.

It was 1834 and in the Vieux Carre some negro boys were playing marbles outside the Old Absinthe House. Down Storyville way girls called Angele, Cecile, Eveline, Celeste and Lola dipped their nipples in sugar water and were topped and tailed by gents from the Garden District.

In Bayou Street, Marie Laveau, the Queen of the Vaudoux, made little hexes from fingernails and menstrual blood. On the corner of Royal Street and Hospital Street, behind a lacy iron grille of cornstalks and flowers and heavy locked cream-coloured shutters, in a dim musty room the smell of clematis and powdered sassafras leaves, Babylon, a coloured slave, was standing beside a stuccoed wall. She was quite naked, her breast pressed against the sweaty white plaster. Her arms were raised over her head and she was on tiptoe due to the fact that her wrists were held in shackles looped over a bracket on the wall.

Madame Marie Dephine McCarty Lalaurie sat listlessly on a chaise longue in the corner of the room. Dipping in a fingerbowl she splashed a little parma violet on her forehead. Sweat seemed to fill the room. From the basement below came the vestige of a gospel chant:

De Lawd he thought he make a man,
Made im o mud an a han full o san.

The refrain was slow and sonorous, rising and falling until the end came together in a jumble:

Dese bones gwin rise agin,
Dese bones gwin rise agin,
Dese bones gwin rise agin,
Brudder, I know'd it, brudder.

In between the verses, Madame Lalaurie listened to the deep heavy breaths of the strained body of her slave. She was irritable in the prickly heat, and unsatisfied.

'Girl, you ain much of a nigger. You don squeal an you aint black.'

For a moment there was silence. Madame Lalaurie shifted to an upright position and felt for her slippers on the parquet floor. She examined the nubile figure of Babylon with a renewed interest. An old appetite, dark and brooding and forbidden, stirred in her stomach until she felt it rise like sweet sickness in her gorge. The chanting continued below:

From dis garden yo mus get,
An earn yo livin by yo sweat.
Dese bones gwin rise agin,
Dese bones gwin rise agin,
Dese bones gwin rise agin,

Brudder, I know'd it, brudder.

She scrutinised the slim, lithe body of Babylon, from just above her knees to the line of her shoulder blades, her coffee skin was striped with a succession of thick plump fiery red welts.

Lalaurie rose and fetched from a corner of the room a slim cane. Daintily she stepped over to the taut figure of Babylon and pressed the end of the cane against the nape of her neck. Babylon pushed her chin into the wall and only let go a little gasp. Her grimace could have been mistaken for a smile, but the dark depths of her eyes squeezed out real hot tears. Slowly, Madame Lalaurie drew the tip of the cane down the line of her backbone, leaving a thin white line through the fiery stripes.

Georgy walked back up Royal Street to the Monteleone Hotel and contemplated the gift of the rose, Blindness will also, he thought, be my gift. One day I will meet myself as a much younger man in these same streets when I will, through the darkness, imagine the mystery lettered in gold on the tiger and the escarlata of the rose. He thought of the words of a German poet, 'the rose has no why, it flowers because it flowers', and of Parcellus, who took the ashes of a rose and, uttering only one word, made it bloom again. He thought of his garden of forking paths in which every story has every outcome conceivable by man and a hundred years could be obliterated in the blink of an eye.

He thought of mirrors and labyrinths, of the caged leopard who could not know that he longed for love and cruelty and the hot pleasure of tearing things to pieces and the scent of a deer. He thought of Dante's Inferno and of man's inhumanity to his fellow man and of the almost animal beauty of the face, which was now unforgettable, of the girl called Charmaine.

He took the rose and placed it in the grillwork of a garden gate. He knew that it would give up its finest scent just before it died. As he slept that night he would dream a single word and a secret miracle that it would presage.

A small breeze blew in from Lake Pontchartrain, and a little dust kicked up along the banquette. The whole city of New Orleans seemed to sink a fraction lower into the swamp, pressing down on the floating corpses in the vaults of the cities of the dead. The sun had set low in the sky and now, as a departing gift, it cast a deep crimson over the river and the old town.

Madame Lalaurie paused in the pursuit of her unusual art and felt the sweat between the creases of her short, plump fingers. Possibly she heard the squeal of a slaughtered chicken or the mumbled litany of a voodoo priest. For a moment she thought that she heard a single word in a language that she did not recognise. She turned to the window from which she detected the sweet sticky scents of the garden. It took her a few seconds to release the catch on the shutters where the bloated veneer had split apart from the frame.

When the red light flooded the room Babylon showed no surprise. As it bathed her naked form and caressed her swollen skin she became whole again. Her grimace was a smile then laughter. The shackles fell and her tears became cold and dropped like miniature jewels. Madame Lalaurie gave only a little grunt and a gurgle as her body was lifted on the crimson flood and floated to the ceiling where her mouth twisted a few times in a last attempt to suck in a breath. But soon there was no more for her to do and her corpse floated in the watery ether as easy as any in the cemetery ovens of New Orleans.

A SHORT HISTORY OF
THE WORD COMPASSION

Compassion (kɒmpæ-ʃɒn), *sb,* [Also **-ioun, -ione, -yon, -scyon.**]

1a. Sympathy, fellow-feeling. *Obs.*

1398 TREVISA *Barth, De P. R.* v. i. (1495) 100 The membres were so sette togyder that... euery one hade compassyon of the other.

1502 HOTTEN *Pandemonium* 5 Compassyone for the Devil maketh much Magick.

1b. Consideration, kindness, mercy. *Obs. Phps Scot.*

1690 KNOX *Sermons* 55 As to compassione, ye are of Stone and not of Flesh. *O Stony hert brake*, for the death of yr Saviour.

1707 UMBERTO *A Discourse on the Composition of Mirrors and the Demons Identified Therein* 293 Being drawn into the mirrors of marble and of ebony, the agonies of those forsaken souls deserved of much compassioun.

1712 J M GOODWILLIE *Northern Wit & Drollerie: mostly p'taining to the Amorous Arts.* vii He felt a compassion when rum-mongering the *Trollope* & rased her *airse* from the cold stone flore.

2. The rigorous and disinterested application of a just and wrathful vengeance. Mercilessness. Hard-heartedness.

1515 COPLAND *The Justice of the Peas* 27 Compassione... not Mercy.

1599 TODD *Antecrist* xli ...he sufferd circunsysyon upon the cros deliverd with grete conpassyon.

1697 *A History of the Sorrows* 355 Compasion deliver'd with the ferocity of Death.

1782 J M BURT *Annals of the Stuarts* II 328 having biggit the machine, he hangit them by the heels, no by the neck, to shew his trew compassion.

1825 BOAG & WESTMACOTT *Sketches from the Prison-House* 32 The compassion of the treadmill, the whipping stool, the oakum picking...

1885 *Athenæum* 20 Jan. 76 He served them after his fashion,/ Witch words laced with compassion...

Last week I discussed the example of simple words, such as 'north' and 'south' that have come to accrue, over centuries, attributes and connotations beyond their simple original meanings.

This week, alternatively, I will deal with a word, like cleave, or fulsome, that has come to have a meaning almost exactly the opposite of its original.

The past, as we say, is a foreign country, and to modern sensibilities the archaic use of the term 'compassion'—to mean mercy and fellow-feeling—is almost stomach-turning in its weakness and cowardice. Of course, we now live in a truly *compassionate* society throughout most of the civilised western world. Most modern states, with the well-quoted historical exceptions in the Middle East and the Balkans, are not content to leave compassion to the discretion of the individual, instead constituting properly state-controlled schedules of pogroms, ethnic-cleansing and punitive tribunals.

The proper place and meaning of compassion in the history of the western world, whilst traceable to the early sixteenth century, is consolidated by the philosophers of the eighteenth century. David Hume, in his *Essay on Man*, makes the clear distinction between the archaic 'sympathy' and the more deliberated term 'empathy'—meaning understanding and taking delight in the suffering of others. Alexander Pope, in the *Dunciad*, eschews the error that human is divine and above the other animals of the earth, suggesting more appropriately rigorous and compassionate models from the animal kingdom. Thus, 'the sagacity of the shark'; 'the imperturbability of the tarantula', 'the consideration of the scorpion'.

The world is shaped by its letters. As Walter Benjamin, one of our most cautionary contemporary critics, notes, 'There can be no Barbarity without Civilisation!'

However, there are also many examples of historical precedent in the application of a compassionate philosophy. One of many examples is that of Patrick Stuart, nephew of Mary Queen of Scots, and Earl of Orkney and Zetland, who exercised a rigorous *compassion* from 1600 to 1620 which was recorded in his diaries.

During this time he exhorted free labour, goods and tributes from his bondsmen for the building of his stronghold and the maintenance of his retinue. His castle, in Scalloway in the Shetland Isles, can still be seen, from the walls of which hang a rusty iron ring. Here, *compassionately*, he would hang those who thwarted his will by the feet (rather than the neck) from dawn to dusk. Few survived this exercise.

Many more examples could be cited of the application of *charity* (another word with archaic antecedents). However, that will be the subject of another column. In conclusion, the best example that I know of the real meaning of compassion can be found in this story, 'The Flyting of Life and Death', from Armstrong's *The Folk-Speech and Tales of Northumbria and Some Districts Adjacent*. I make no apology for including it in its entirety.

Some years ago, the story goes, the burghers of Anwickdale and Carrickside had announced a grand flyting on the festival of Guid Neeburris. A flyting was a competition of words, in which the finest rhymers and singers of tales would vie to produce the most sublime words. This they would do not through the weak and effeminate gestures of malison, or goodwill, but through benison, in which they could berate and insult their opponent.

The flyting was to be between the finest of the local bards and singers, Tammas Truisdale, a good northern man—steadfast as northern rock and as firm as a winter forest—a man of delightful invention and wit, whose cants and ballads had spread from shore to shore, and a stranger, who had come from afar with reports of his wisdom and ways with words. It was whispered that the stranger was called the Walking Man—for he had no abode on this earth other than the hearth and the porage bowl that he could earn nightly through his songs. And it was whispered that he had come from the other side of the world and that he had walked in the desert at the hour when the cold night and the hot sun had not decided who should rule and he had travelled through valleys that were cut by rivers like knives. His songs and tales, so it was said, came not from mortal man, but from the reflections of demons in watery stones and fiery ice. In anticipation of the stranger and his louche and uncanny southern ways, the burghers were afire with trepidation and fascination.

The flyting, it being a grand festival and feast day, was no simple flyting. It was to be nothing less than a flyting of life and death, the most wonderful instrument that the bards had devised, from many years of practice and of consideration. All the burghers, the bird-scarers, the coppicers, the cordswainers, the cold-smiths, the bakers, the bagmen, the wattlers, the wives, the winnowers, the journeymen, the tailors, the soutars, the ploughmen and anyone else from near or far had come to see the contest.

The stranger sang first, of life. And he sang so beautifully that his song felt like the damp sand that sticks to your bare toes in the morning, like the little eruptions of crystals of overnight snow, like the scent of cherry when the blossom is waiting to fall. He sang so excellently that all the listeners were lost in a reverie and failed to notice time itself passing by and the hour of death ticking ever closer.

Then it was the turn of Tammas. And as he sang he derided and scorned life and the Walking Man. He sang of death so fluidly as to turn his song of death into a carrion crow. He made it into a canker that bit at the flimsy belly of the song of life. He made it into a chilly wind that, in an evening of sad unsettled skies, when a door bangs shut and a mangy dog howls in the distance and the night conspires against sleep, creeps through a crevice and settles, unwelcome, by the fireside.

Now, it so happened that Death himself was in the audience

that night. He was hidden and cowled, although his face, if viewed upside down or in a mirror, formed a figure or heiroglyph that spelled terror to mortal men.

Death mused at the songs and tales and at the ferocity of the flyting and at the exposition of death against life, but while he did so he planned new and pleasing ways to continue his feud with life.

Then the judges retired to consider their verdict which, when duly considered, was such: that the stranger had sung eloquently indeed of life, and had conjured magnificently and with skill and meaning, but that the song of death had answered the song of life and had dulled its brilliance with its deathly certainty and its hard clear core.

And the Walking Man applauded Tammas and granted that his song was indeed the finest of songs of death. However, he humbly requested, before he took the road, that Tammas accept another flyting. This time a flyting of love, a noble subject for ballad and song.

Tammas agreed to the flyting and began his song of love. He sang of love that was endless and absolute. That lovers needed their love like the rain needs the flood, like the lock needs the key, like the axe needs the log and the wind needs the tree.

For a time, Death listened to the song, and, for once, his heart was touched and he no longer felt the bitter blood coursing in his veins. For a little while he almost forgot his purpose and in the tenderness of the song almost thought that he could refrain from his calling and embrace life itself.

Then the Walking Man said he would continue and that he would not need to swagger or dissemble or counter his opponent through scorn or derision. He said that he would sing *simply* of love, but that it would no longer be love in life, but love in death. And so he began to sing.

And he sang of the true measure of love as loss. Of love that in the absolution of its end posits no beginning, love that in its darkness extinguishes all light. He sang of love unto death and the death of love as if they were one. And his song reached into the hearts of all who heard it and made their hearts cold and slow and chilled their bones to the marrow.

He sang of how in love's loss all that was touched would wither in blight, of endless dreams that would murder sleep, of ideas unrealised and songs unsung and of the things that would fester and wither in the shadow of love unrequited. He sang of how love could long for death and death remain oblivious to love. He sang of love that sucks death into its deep pink wound, of love as liquid fire. Of love that twists its faith into turmoils of desire. Of love at the edges, love in rot and rust, love that wavers at the margins and loses everything for a moment of mistrust.

Of all this he sang, and more, and sang until he had squeezed the song of love in life of its last drop of joy or goodness.

And death, hearing this, as his tears wept blood, realised the significance of his deathly cause and its transcendance of love. In the earthly world, the crowd gasped in awe and wonder as his body fell apart in a rattling of bones, but in the sublime world, his ferocity and *compassion* [my italics] in imparting his duty was greater than even he could have imagined.

THE ANTI-VITRUVIAN

The following papers were collected at the Pitt Street headquarters of Strathclyde Police during January-July 2000, and are accurately transcribed. The majority of the papers had previously been in the collection of Shena Gordon, journalist, late of 27 Marchmont Gardens, Kelvinside. The papers constitute a live investigation file. Although some are in the public domain, they are not for general release in their current form.

(1) Feature article by Shena Gordon, *The Independent Scot*, 9th March 2019:

GO-AHEAD FOR CONTROVERSIAL NEO-TENEMENT

The planning committee, chaired by Sir Simpson Fraser, for Glasgow's Year of Architecture and Design (scheduled for 2022) announced yesterday that they have given the go ahead for Crawfurd J Fargan's controversial Neo-Tenement project. The £5M project flies in the face of the powerful 1990 Group who campaigned for a low cost, environmental and community-oriented approach to the event.

The purpose of the project is described by Fargan, Scotland's most vaunted twentieth-century architect as 'to capture the sculptural essence of the Glasgow tenement over two centuries.' It will occupy a prime site on the corner of Renfrew Street and Rose Street. Construction is planned to commence next month.

Pip Hayward, consultant editor of the avant-garde art and architecture journal *Continuum*, one of a minority of critics in support of the project, described it as 'a huge opportunity for

Scottish design to spearhead the conceptualist movement into the new millennium following the lead of Johnny Rodger whose 'drawing machine' realisation of Mackintosh's unbuilt Art School has heralded a new form of architecture.' However, Rob Forsyth, arts editor of *The Scot on Sunday* and one of Fargan's staunchest critics, called the Neo-Tenement, 'potentially the most monstrous architectural birth of this or any other century, shamefully planned to herald the new millennium in Scotland.'

(2) Extract from an interview by Shena Gordon with Crawfurd J Fargan, *The Scot on Sunday*, 25th April 1999:

SG: Crawfurd, despite your huge success and international reputation, you have powerful enemies who have dubbed your work the New Brutalism and attack its sustainability. What do you say to them?

CJF: Well, I can say to them: is the rose brutal because of the nature of its thorns? What I have tried to do with my work is seek the beauty in the sculptural forms of intransigent materials such as concrete and stone. It is not an art that is aimed merely at prettification, it is an art that is pure within itself. Goethe called architecture 'frozen music'. My architecture aims towards that mobilisation of material. A stone is not only a stone. It is a geometry of planes and angles that can explode into meaning.

SG: But are buildings not for people to inhabit, to feel comfortable and at ease in?

CJF: Did people feel completely at ease in the great cathedrals of the Renaissance? Or in the tower blocks of the Machine Age, or in the corridors of commerce and finance? The answer is, of course, not always. Some great architecture makes us feel subservient and weak.

SG: Is that not at the crux of the criticism of your new work? Some critics suggest that it is, is essence, the architecture of cruelty and sadism.

CJF: OK... one way to answer that is this. Of all the great architectural products of the industrial era, how many of them have bowed to the mere machinery of the human body. Was the Seminary, the Infirmary, the Mill, the Panopticon built to merely accommodate the body or to discipline and control it. In the crazy logic of the Carceri where is the comfort or the beauty? Yet, think of it... is it not possible there is a greater beauty in the awesome size and scope of it all?

SG: But is this single-mindedness not overly self-indulgent? Especially, in the light of current circumstances, for a city that faces so many economic and social problems?

CJF: Perhaps, but our purpose is not to pander merely to society's concerns, it is to produce an architectural question mark that will begin to serve an argument around the nature of society and self. It is intended as an icon of current architectural thought, as was the Bauhaus in its time or as is the Millennium Pseudo-dome more recently.

SG: But surely your latest project is not in that category, since it is based on the tenement—which was, was it not, housing for the masses?

CJF: The Neo-Tenement is not housing, it is a poetic statement based on a form of housing. It is the quiddity of the tenement realised not only in the quantities of space and volume which the architect freely possesses as his own domain, but also in the quantities of the senses, of sight and smell, and even of time.

SG: Crawfurd, there are many Glaswegians of our own generation, like both you and I, who were brought up in tenements. Sometimes in conditions of poverty and squalor. They have memories—some happy, some sad. Some long for the return of the tenement but most don't mourn its demise. How will they feel about the Neo-Tenement?

CJF: I don't know how they will feel. They may feel elation, they may feel terror. If they feel as I do about it they may feel that it is the essence of all that they are. It may be their dreams or their nightmares. It may last for a fleeting moment or stand still in time. There are no half measures. What I want is for the future to say that this is (was) architecture (art) at its rawest. If I achieve that, then I will have succeeded.

(3) Letter to Shena Gordon, late of 27 Marchmont Gardens, Kelvinside, postmarked 5th May 2018:

Dear Ms Gordon [The name is written in blue ink],

I write to thank you for your perceptive interview... I especially enjoyed discussing our childhood experiences of the tenements; my memories of Dalmarnock, as you know, and yours of Dennistoun.

I think it could be mutually beneficial for us to meet and discuss some of the issues further. I sometimes use a bar called the Hotspur in Drury Street. It is invariably busy and therefore private...

[The paper is torn off at this point.]

(4) Extract from *The Vitruvian Fallacy*, independently published by C J Fargan (Glasgow, 1999):

> 'It is the light of order and not the darkness of chaos
> that is truly imprisoning.'
>
> Piranesi
>
> 'Be Cruel!'
>
> Foucault

The anti-Vitruvian is not just cerebral but also visceral.

The anti-Vitruvian does not pander to the inexact architecture of the human body or form.

The anti-Vitruvian is for the individual, not the horde.

The anti-Vitruvian has no manifesto, only a will to create.

The anti-Vitruvian has no credo, only a need to state.

The anti-Vitruvian eschews history in favour of memory, nostalgia in favour of reverie, sentimentality in favour of pain.

Vitruvius, from *De architectura libri decem* (31BC): 'In architecture, as in all the other Operative Arts, the End must direct the Operation. The End is to build well. Well building hath three conditions, Commodity, Firmness and Delight.'

The Anti-Vitruvian, from *The Vitruvian Fallacy* (2019AD): 'In architecture, as in all the other Operative Arts, the End must direct the Operation. The End is to build true. True building hath three conditions, Incommodity, Intransigence and Consternation.'

(5) Page of a notebook formerly belonging to Shena Gordon:

Memories: the middens, nits (the nit nurse), the briquette (spelling?) man, sannies, creepy-crawlies in the toilet (earywigs?), the rag and bone man (Scottish name for this?), Pat Roller and Lobey Dosser, dreeping off dykes, caurs...

[The above is interpersed among various doodles of indeterminate meaning.]

(6) Review of *The Anti-Vitruvian*, independently published by C J Fargan (Glasgow, 2019) by R W Forsyth, *Scottish Books in Review,* No. 33 (August, 2020):

Despite the largely undeserved reputation of its putative author, this farrago of inconsequential extravagances will be largely ignored by the architectural community in Scotland. It offers nothing to the series of constructive debates that surround Glasgow's privileged position as City of Architecture and Design in the forthcoming millennial year. It is neither founded on an examined history and tradition of design and construction nor is it based on a philosophical principle other than the crudest form of self-aggrandisement. Whatever whim or fancy may have triggered this work it cannot be said to reveal anything other its author's delusions of power as some sort of architectural übermensch unbeholding to any authority or agency or, indeed, the public, who ultimately pay for his deluded and unproductive work.

(7) Poem, extracted from *The Glasgow Academical,* Vol. 1, no. 2 (1965):

> Baby fat forged from memory's desire,
> That moment present and already gone
> Will future me, foundry me
> From a dry gasp of Glasgow words.
> Hopes of a lost empire of stone,
> The lead grey rod of a buried canal,
> A ballad of books yet to be unread,
> The consequential friction
> Of two opposing football teams.
>
> Testaments of a Golden City:
> A perambulation in boyish rags,
> Starling roost and scorching rain.
> Sooted, screeching streets of
> Lattice tattie bags
> And blind, Pay-packeted

Bunnets of men.

Branded father red and mother blue,
The once and future maybe me,
Tenemented to be, and not yet lost,
While this fat-fest fool machine,
Schools the future and suborns the past.

W J Fargan

(8) Extract from a paper delivered by Crawfurd J Fargan to the Royal Institute of Scottish Architects. Published in *Scottish Architectural Review*, Vol. XIX (2017):

Tenementum means nothing other than a plot of land for building on—which is the fundamental requirement of every architectural project. But the tenement has come to mean something else. It has been lauded by artists, such as Morrison, Whone, Eardsley and Paton and writers who generally see its manifestations through some distorting lens of nostalgia. For example, Guy McCrone, a mediocre novelist, referred to 'the misty smoke and the tenements of Glasgow [which] caught in the light, made a magic of their own'.

The tenement supposedly has a cultural history which is set out by Frank Arneil Walker:

The tenement is woven into the fabric of Glasgow, held fast in the 'pleached alleys' that cross and re-cross the urban landscape… All too frequently, a roseate (sic) view of the tenement's fancied past or a bitter consciousness of the squalor and despair that have sometimes afflicted its old age, has become the basis for appraisals of architecture and townscape as critically fallacious as Ruskin's Victorian moralising that men must be good else they could not paint… [some] have pictured the tenemented streets of the city as prison walls behind which an exploited society exercised its grim existence, denied, adulterated, diluted, cowed.

And it has been mooted as not just an architectural category but a 'way of life'. Thus, the tenement as a concept falls within the province of the writer, the painter, the sociologist and the photographer as well as the architect and planner. However, the tenement must exist other than as a metaphor, a shorthand for an experience or a form of categorisation of the society it existed within. The tenement must have a form, a feel, an essence. Eventually, it will comprise a mechanism that creates meaning free from representation.

My Neo-Tenement will exist out of history, out of tradition, out of nostalgia. It will return to the essence of the tenemental form. It will reveal itself only to those who are willing to divest themselves of their preconceptions and approach their experience anew—as for the first time.

My Neo-Tenement will only reveal its hidden secrets to the adult-child, or the child-adult, among us. Gibbon, reputedly, felt giddy and sick when confronted with the glories of the Roman Empire. Edwin Muir and Lewis Grassic Gibbon describe the same symptoms when confronted with the glory of Glasgow, its tenement slums. The sociologist, Ian Simpson, writes that 'living in a slum for a child is a strange mixture of revulsion and wonder. Slums are hemmed in by their backyards and middens—places where all that we divest returns to its elemental state, borderlands between nature and culture.'

My Neo-Tenement will encompass a sweet sickness that will speak to those of us appalled at the hypocrisy and banality of Scottish society. I think of Walpole's critique of Piranesi: ' …

he imagined scenes that would startle geometry and exhaust the Indies to realise. He piled palaces on bridges and temples on palaces, and scaled heaven with mountains of edifices. What taste was in his boldness! What grandeur in his rashness and details!'

The Neo-Tenement will encompass such ambition, if it comes to be realised at all. Perhaps some of us will live to see the day; some will not…

(9) Notes from a page of a jotting pad apparently taken by Shena Gordon subsequent to a meeting with Crawfurd J Fargan:

Thursday, Hotspur Bar [In red ink, no date given.]

The MIRACLE of the Gorbals.
The DARK-SIDE of Glasgow.
The CHANGING-FACE of the City.
The MEMORY of Concrete.
The RECOVERY of Childhood.
The REFLECTION of Stone.
The GRANDNESS of the Dichotomy.
The FISHINESS of the King.
The PRESENCE of the Past.
The FINALITY of the Future.
The APPROPRIATENESS of the End…

(10) Obituary for Crawfurd J Fargan, *The Independent Scot,* 2nd January 2020:

The world-renowned architect, Crawfurd J Fargan, died suddenly and in mysterious circumstances on his seventieth birthday. Tragically, only months before the unveiling of his latest and most controversial project—the Neo-Tenement, flagship of Glasgow's year of Architecture and Design.

Born in Dalmarnock on 14th February 1951 and christened William James, Fargan—known to his friends as Billy—adopted the Christian name of his maternal great-grandfather in his professional life. His family; his father an ironworker at St Rollox, his mother and two sisters, were among the first to be decanted from the decaying tenements to the pristine Moss Heights complex in Cardonald.

Fargan won a scholarship to Glasgow Academy and shone academically, latterly studying at Glasgow School of Art and the Royal Academy. He joined the London company of Haworth Monk and achieved prominence in the eighties with a string of projects which boldly resisted the excesses of the postmodern school: notably Clerkenwell's Ainslie Green housing project, the 'Bleachers' at Glasgow Green, Luton Hatters community pavilion, and the Sean Connery Museum at Marbella. Since 1990, however, all his projects have been conceptual.

Although Fargan graced the international stage, he never forgot his Scottish roots, proclaiming as his architectural antecedents not only Mendelsohn's Einsteinturm in Potsdam, Taut's die Stadtkrone, and Roger's Heaven Harbour Complex in Hong Kong, but also Mackintosh's unbuilt Glasgow School of Art, Thomson's St Vincent Street Church, Spence's Queen Elizabeth Square, and Hadid's Edinburgh Millennium Pseudo-dome.

Fargan is survived by a wife and daughter (estranged for several years).

The Neo-Tenement will be reviewed in the Arts and Culture section in four weeks time. We await a further statement on the circumstances surrounding the death of Crawfurd J Fargan.

(11) Letter to Shena Gordon, late of 27 Marchmont Gardens, Kelvinside, postmarked 31st December 2019:

Dear Shena [The name is written in blue ink],

Please accept this invitation to review the Neo-Tenement on behalf of the *Independent Scot*. You invitation is as dated below. A press pack is included. I will, unfortunately, not be available on the day in question.

The peculiar nature of the Neo-Tenement allows only access to one viewer at a time. In deference to our considerations on the matter, I have decided to allow the *Independent Scot* the privilege of first viewing of the project.

Crawfurd J Fargan [Signed in blue ink.]

(12) Transcript of a tape recording (undetermined date). The voice is identified as that of Shena Gordon, late of 27 Marchmont Gardens, Kelvinside:

I enter the Neo-Tenement by way of an outside stairway built on the side of the hill (the drumlins run north to south across the city following the scars of forgotten glaciers). The sandstone facade, prematurely greyed, rises above me into the clouds. The steps seem to be unnaturally sized, and project outwards like wedges. The first is too high to stretch. My foot slips—heel sparking on the polished grey stone. I realise that I should have worn my black-soled sandshoes. Now I have scraped my knee beneath my skirt and my hands are dirty and gritted from gripping the next step. The effect of the sloping steps seems to be to push me out of the stairway. I imagine falling down the steps onto the hill, and a pram careering down and overturning (is this my imagination or some distant memory?)

I grab the eroded edge of the close entrance and pull myself into a dark corridor. There is a closehead gas mantle (unlit) and chipped white tiles on the walls with stained brown cracks.

Further down dark shadows narrow to a slatted black door. Some daylight escapes through the uneven slats.

Turning left I mount the first flight of stairs with echoing footsteps. There is a sort of surrounding silence punctuated by half-heard sounds from hollow pipes. Somewhere around me there must be the veins and arteries of plumbing and draining. I think there is a faint smell of escaping gas.

I am alone, but I turn nervously, imagining a surreptitious footfall at my back.

I am progressing up the steps. My feet slip neatly into worn depressions in the age-old stone. But the steps seem to get larger and more concave and I stretch to reach the first floor landing.

The space is at first confined, but also seems to open out above (where I cannot reach) into a murky vagueness. There is a window of opaque thick glass, with side panels stained tobacco brown. The panes are flaking; painted wood rotted into the stone. It is impossibly high and I strain to put my ear to the cold dusty glass. But I hear nothing, there is no sign of the external world. I discover that I am buttressed on my right by a heavy wooden coal bunker with broken rusty hinges and the door to the outside lavatory on the left. I try to raise the lid of the bunker to peer inside (God knows why) but it is too heavy to raise more than a couple of inches.

Then I drop it with a start and my heart pounds. There is a sound from behind the lavatory door. Panicking I press my back against the bunker and reluctantly face the decaying green toilet door. It is thick, ill-fitting with a unfeasibly large keyhole.

I reassure myself. It is only plumbing noises. But I can't bring myself to put my hand to the door (and certainly not my eye to the peephole.)

Then I think I see something black, in the corner of my eye, scurrying across the landing floor.

I close my eyes then I open them again to clear a watery film.

I steady myself. Then I move decisively and steadily ascend the stairs to the next landing. It is more commodious here, and the gas mantles are lit. I can see, in the flickering light, that there are three doors to each landing. They are solid and dark, like an obstacle, not an entrance. I peer at the brass nameplates on each door. The first says 'Imagine the City', the second 'Let Glasgow Flourish—by telling the truth!' The third is scratched and the strokes of the letters half-blacked. I can just make it out—'haec autem ita fieri debent, ut habeatur ratio firmitatis, utilitatis, venustasis'—but I don't have time to translate it, even vaguely, from my schoolgirl Latin.

The lights suddenly fade. I feel cold, as if I am pursued by a darkness from below and behind. I decide to ascend to the next landing, but my legs are wearying, and I struggle to make any progress, as if my feet are sinking into the folds of the soft stone. I push myself forwards and, grabbing the rim of the last gigantic step, mantleshelf onto the landing.

But the darkness seems thick and all encompassing here. I reach forward expecting to feel the comparative warmth of a panelled door, but there is nothing... nothing! So I swing around and decide to descend the staircase and exit. I tell myself I am not panicking, but I am keeping hidden inside my adult body a child's compunction to flee and escape.

Then I realise that the steps beneath my feet are damp and slippy. Some light seems to enter—from above—and it is natural daylight, not gaslight. There is a slight breeze and then I hear the sound of dripping water. As my eyes accustom themselves to the darkness I realise that I am in a massive stairwell defined by a plummeting spiral staircase bordered with twisted rusty iron rails. The black circular centre of the stairwell falls away to nothingness. Water is dripping into its dark core. The light reflects on a few drops as they fall.

My feet are slipping on the cold wet stone, and I suddenly feel as if I am being pushed by the slippery slope into the centre. I reach out and touch one of the iron rails but a piece of rust flakes off in my hand and the whole thing moves with a creak.

I sit on the step, feeling its solidity for a moment, as the damp soaks through my skirt and into my pants. There is nothing else for it. I remove my shoes and, pressing against the outer wall of the spiral, as carefully as I can, more sliding than walking, make my way down the staircase, not knowing what awaits me at the bottom.

I pant and choke a little. The sound of the water has stopped and I can hear my own breathing and heartbeat. There is a distinct, unpleasant smell, like burnt cabbage, and my feet no longer feel the steps. I have reached the bottom.

As I rise to my feet, I see a familiar pattern, the slatted door facing me is the same that I saw when I first entered the close. Yet there is only darkness behind me now. I go to the door, lift a heavy iron latch and swing it open towards me. I see the sky, some darkening clouds scudding above me, I have left the tenement and I am in the backcourt.

There is all around the smell of rubbish and decay. Massive bins in their own dirty houses overflow with all manner of scraps and leftovers, liquid and solid. These are secondhand signs of human habitation—there are no others. I ascend a few steps. On a level with my chin the ground, where puddles have worn the stone away, is damp. I can put my finger into a smooth black cream, mud darkened with chimney smoke and soot. This is the uncompromising paste from which little children once made pies.

The compound I am in is but one amongst many others, all of irregular shapes, as if they had not so much been planned as fought over. They are all at different levels and the boundaries are massive stone dykes, some capped with finished stone, others open and raw, with a few dandelions and other weeds growing in cracks. High above and in the distance, are the pock-marked stone walls of tenements, some buttressed with external stairwells, all topped with ranks of chimneys and pitted with dark unyielding windows.

There is the distant squawk of a seagull. The clouds are darkening and the winds blows through my skirts and sodden legs. I feel cold. I don't want to be alone in this wilderness in the dark.

But then I sense something, some movement. As it darkens, I think I can make out a shape. Then I focus a little more. I think it is the shape of a little girl in a cotton dress. She nimbly jumps on top of a stone dyke and dreeps down into the next courtyard.

But then I'm not sure. What was this ghostly ephemeral shape? But I feel compelled to follow. I clamber onto the dyke and scrape my knees, wiping the stinging blood with the unblackened back of my hand. I don't stop to think but drop with a thud to the ground. The shock shivers through my body and my little bare feet feel the pin pricks of the gravelly ground.

Ahead of me I can make out another slatted door. It swings a little, unevenly on its hinges in the wind. From inside escapes a little light, ephemeral but warming against the cold wind at my back.

I enter another close. There is a stairway and at its bottom a door, panelled rather than flush but bare, unevenly, as if it has been stripped of its paint with a blowtorch. Beside the door, the source of an almost sickly yellow light, is a barred window of glass as thick as bottle bottoms. The window, however, is at ground level, starting at about the height of my waist and seemingly continuing below ground, through the floor of the close.

I stand with my back to the far wall, staring at this gaunt yellow eye. Is this where ghosts go? The horror of the empty halls, the uncanny shuffling and scuttling of the tenement around me comes back with a flood. I imagine I hear singing or keening noises in the distance, behind the mottled door. Lost in fear and fascination I reach forward...

[Although the tape continues recording for some time, it is not possible to discern individual human voices.]

(13) Extract from feature article by Rob Forsyth, *The Independent Scot*, 1st July 2000:

DEMISE OF CONTROVERSIAL NEO-TENEMENT

The Planning Committee of Glasgow District Council today finally pulled the plug on the controversial Neo-Tenement project devised by the late Crawfurd J Fargan. Since the much publicised and sensational events surrounding the architect's death and the dismissal, amidst accusations of graft and corruption, of the entire board of the Operations Section of the Year of Architecture and Design, there has been little public support for the venture.

Sir Simpson Fraser, chair of the Committee, stated publicly last week that the unsightly work in progress deserved to take over from the National Monument on Calton Hill as 'Scotland's Shame'. The site, it was announced, is being considered for the proposed new Scottish Museum of Industry and Commerce. Family and friends of the architect were unavailable for comment.

(14) Poem, printed on an extracted leaf (pages 11-12) from a volume identified by a pencil inscription in the margin as *Hallucinations and Other Poems* (New Foulis Press, 1975):

[The title is obscured by black ink.]

One night I dreamed a door,
Paint-flaked and panelled.
An oil can's worth of creak,

Its letter-box in Latin,
Its nameplate bronzed in Greek.
I stiffly turned the handle,
Stepped in, pulled flush the door.
Blackness was the ceiling,
Blackness was the floor.
Instinct mothered panic,
I grasped into the air,
For a light-switch never thought of,
On a wall that wasn't there.

So I knew my will to dream,
Must dream itself a room.
Windowed chintz and chiffon,
A clock upon the wall,
Carpeted Axminster,
An entrance from a hall.
I added several others,
Dark architect of rooms.
I corked them with a chimney,
I capped them with a roof
Some were warm and friendly,
Some haughty and aloof.
I sought an artist's purpose,
I sought a poet's rhyme,
I sought a frank opinion;
But the rooms could not agree,
Each kept its own dominion
And measured its own time.
Each whispered with desire
And kept its mullioned spies,
As if it was a blind man,
With ambitious, eager eyes.

The end's a soft awakening,
A footfall on a strand.
My abode by nightfall,
My hopeless, ill-starred plan,
Got up and walked away!
The whole accursed shebang.
Dreams are made of shadows,
Of labyrinths, and of sand.
I thought I dreamed a house,
In fact, I'd dreamt...
[The end of the line is obscured by black ink.]

W (C) J F

[No published work entitled *Hallucinations and Other Poems* can be located in the catalogues of the British Library, the National Library of Scotland or the Mitchell Library.]

THE WORLD TURNED
UPSIDE DOWN

Nature sowed the seed of chaos and of light,
To blot out Order, extinguish gentle Night;
Monsters rose from swirling mists,
To curse the apple Eve had kiss'd.

Alexander Pope

He who would fight with monsters must take care not to become one.

Friedrich Nietxsche

I am Jonathan Blunt, God help me, of Fareham, in the Countie of Hampshire. I am not Privy to the world of Pycture, nor to the world of Romance. I am a Simpleman and I will tell my Historie in strait Wordes as well I can it. *Habent sua fata libella.*

It was in the Year of our Saviour seventeen hundred and twenty. As was my way on occasiones, I was seat'd in St James. My penny was at the Bar and I sippt coffee with ginger and honie. Mr. St. John Toast was there, Sir Andrew Fontaine, and Mr. Alex. Pope, the Papist, and Sir Richard Steele. Altho the place was, at this tyme, unsurpass'd for Wit and Drollerie, there was a cold Cloude in the air, for many had been undone by the South Sea religione.

Since none of the Geniuses would speke, I thought to discourse on the Subjects I had mynded at the Moment: Dr Harvey's *Exercitatio Anatomica* and the circulation of the bloud, Wm. Buchan's regimen for Diseases, and the Case that had been discover'd at Godlamyng, where a WOMAN had borne seventeen Rabbets or parts of Rabbets and it was sayd that the longing of a WOMAN that had not conceiv'd could Mark the Infant in the WOMB with the MARK of that they long'd for.

This led to some talk of Monsters, and I spoke of the sinnes of Debauchery, Onanism, Whoredom, Adulterie and Fornication, and other Sodomiticall sinnes of uncleanness that did so outrageously raign, and of the anatomy of Abuses that were the causes of such Monstrous births recently enumerated. To whit: Consanguinity or Affinitie of the Bloud; the Diseases hereditrarie; Over-Abundance of Seed; Confusion of Seed of divers Kinds; Bestial Coupling, or, the WOMAN atop the man; a WOMAN in Conception afright'd by a Creature.

When I was but halfway engag'd upon this Discourse, I saw that the Company were intent upon some Dripps on the Stones of the Flore. For my periwig had wilt'd in the winter rain, and was all forsaken, sodden and soggy, which caus'd grete Hilaritie. Mr. Pope then coin'd an epigram for it:

> True Wit is Nature to Advantage drest,
> Which oft is Thought, but rarely well exprest,
> So Dr Blunt, forsaken all that's said,
> To whet his Tongue, has soak'd his Head.

I berat'd them for their un-Godliness, where-upon Sir Richard, who was versed in Bawdry (and some said keeped Companie with the Hermaphrodites in the Molly-Houses) made a filthy Verse in the Stile of the infamous Rochester:

> Poor Dr Blunt,
> His pintle ne'er has rived a C____,
> If sermon-making comes to Pass,
> His righteous Pen would draw an A___!

I call'd him for the Monsters in the sea and all the Buffoons, Newsmongers, Quacks, Projectors, Effeminates, Detractors and Oafs that ever had been seen in the Smyrna, Jerusalem, Garraway's, Button's, Pasqua Rosee's, the Bay Tree, the Turk's Head, &c.

Sir Andrew then interject'd and sade Pray hold your Tongue, good Jonathan, for you are indeed our best Physician and the Nonpareil of Discoursers on Monsters. In fact, he continu'd, The only Dr that knows more of Monsters than our Dr is Dr Swift, the mad parson. I was appeas'd by his Contribution and retir'd to my lodgings.

⧗

With my Fingers I squeez'd the point'd PAPS of the breasts to see they were fit for Suckling, whilst Mr. Browne check'd for the Common Evacuations.

The very next day after the Discourse at St James, I had taken the chain mail to Godlamyng where Mr. Browne, the Bone-Setter had call'd me to examine the RABBET-WOMAN. Remembering the Experiment of Dr William Harvey who had disguis'd himself as a Wizard to meet a Witch and then had opened up the belly of her Familiar, a toad, to shew that it was just an arrant ordinary toad, I had consign'd myself to the application of Science to this Legend.

At Quarter before Twelve, the WOMAN fell into fresh Labour-panes, beginning a-new to cry out very strangely. I keeped her Knees close together; and holding my Head against her Head , I took her Hands into myne, whilst she stooping with her Head forwards, push'd her Back against the Back of the Chair with such Violence, that I was forc'd to hold the Chair to prevent its tumbling over. she repeated the same afterwards at two or three different Times. Those Panes being gone off, Mr. Browne examin'd her again, and then suffer'd me to do the same, which accordingly I did. Upon touching her, I presently perceiv'd some broken Bones, and advancing with my Finger unto the Orifice of the VAGINA, I discover'd a fleshy Body, which with the bones stood a littel way out. The VAGINA was contract'd, close embracing the Body, which presented itself, and which I conjectur'd to be the hind Part of a Rabbet, strippt of the Fur.

The extreme Dryness of the Parts, the strong Contraction of the VAGINA, and the Apprehension I was under, lest the Fore-Part should be in the same Condition with that I felt, made me proceed with some Caution, insomuch that I resolved rather to wait the Return of new Labour-panes, than by using any Violence, to tear and to injure the VAGINA.

Having retired for these Reasons, Mr. Browne ask'd me, whether I would not extract it; and upon my answering No, he offer'd to make it easier for me, pretending, that his Fingers were slenderer than mine: Accordingly he examin'd her, and presently desir'd me to touch her again, which I did, and found the Body abovesaid advanced a little way; but when I laid hold of it, the VAGINA contracted itself so strongly, that it snapp'd back again full the Breadth of a finger. I jump'd myself away, Afrighted. The Mr. Browne put his Hands into the Orifice and pull'd out a Shape and then he gave it to me. The Shape was Head (or rather the Skull) of a Beast, but strippt of the Skin, and where there were socketts for the Eyes, there was just a littel Substance, red like Bloud.

And Mr. Browne sade that never in the World of Romance had he rede of such a Wonderfull site

And I sade Truly that not a Necromancer, who can rase Spirits from a Stone, could conjour such a Monster.

And we Retir'd and Pray'd to God for the WOMAN and the unnattural Childe or *What-God-Will*, not knowing what Mockery was to await us (for, as it happen'd, we were most horribly *Gull'd*, for the WOMAN had put the bits into Herself at grete pane, and Mr. Browne and I were Sorely ridicul'd and scorn'd by the People for it.

⧗

Mistress Handsell sade pore Master Blunt, for the Moone has surely drawn a Tide of Bloud from you, like a Woman in Rags.

And I lookt at Myself in the Looking-glass and I was all

a-trembling and white like a cloude. I sade this Daye has leech'd the Bloud from me and I am a *Muffet* or a *Fool*.

I had taken the lodging at Godlamyng for a seven-day in Expectance of much more Invention which would not come to pass.

The gudewoman bade me sit and I benefit'd much from the application of Vinegar, but that Daye was not well done yet, for when I retir'd, and remov'd my Gloves, the Hands that had enter'd the WOMAN were all redden and rough and caus'd me to crye out, thus bringing muche Distress to the House and the CHAMBERMAID came upon me and on seeing my head in BAND-AGE and my hands in SALVE did insolently Laugh at my DISTRESS.

And I kept my tongue at rest although I knew the sins of Lechery and Venery and that young Girls, the Divell having enter'd their Mynd, would Flit and Fall off againe, oftimes getting a great Bellie by some lustfull Match, and, I will confesse, many young Men, through the heate and strength of Concupisence, have most shamefully abus'd, both Widdowes and Maydens. I sayed so much to Mistress Handsell and I curs'd the RABBET-WOMAN and call'd her a most slipperie Eele, for deceiving us. And Mistress Handsell sade God forgive the pore WOMAN, for she had borne a Childe without Eye-lids, which was itself a Monster, and since then had been Distract'd.

Then Mistress Handsell ask'd me if she could oblige to send the Servant to me, to be Beaten, for her Mischief.

But I declin'd, for I was Tired, and I had no Apetite for such sports that cause the Bloode to heat unnaturally and provok'd impure thoughts.

Then she bid me to stay CALM, for she saw that I was still arous'd and she sade that I had dwelt with the WOMAN too long. And I sade that I could not but stay as I was there in the pursuit of WISDOM.

Perhaps then, she sade, I should see someone who could absolve me of my Discomfort and she sade that the Wisest man in alle these parts was a Jonathan also, and that his name was Dr Swift.

I start'd at this, for was this not the Dr Swift that knew of Monsters, as I was apprais'd by Sir Andrew Fontaine?

Thereupon that next morning, I arose and made my way on the back of a beast I had hir'd, to the Hog's Back, through the townes of SEALE and BADSHOT LEA and past Mother Carey's Cave until I came to the HIGH MILL, whereabout I stopp'd by the water of the WEY and sat awhile while I watch'd the Heron and the Halcyon sport.

The House of Dr Swift was less than one Mile from there and as I approach'd it I discern'd that it sat gracefully in a field in which there were HORSES of various colours. I gently and in quiet entered through the field so as not to disturb the BEASTS.

Dr Swift grett'd me himself as it seem'd that he was all alone in the LOBBY of the grate house. Of Dr Swift it could be sayd that he was of Portly demeanour and of sound *BODY* not a lump of deformity like Mr Pope with his brent back. He seem'd AMENIABLE enough.

I discount'd to him the Storie of the WOMAN of Godlydamning and the dreadful Sham it constituted. He did not seem to shew that Indignation that a man of Matters should shew to see a Fellow so shoddilly gull'd. For rather, he laugh'd and sade that the WOMAN had a Wit herself to so fool such Eminences and Geniuses.

I was perhaps not too well pleas'd with this, but he bid me PARDON him for he sayd that his was not a HOUSE for to visit in Publick, but was instead a contrary HOUSE for in it I would see *The World Turn'd Upside Down.*

Not all Things on Earth can be seen in the Sun. I will shew to you Pictures that are dark and gloomie and of Shaddowes that can Alone be seen by the Moone-lighte. Thus I will provide for you an *Enlighten-ment*.

He light'd seven Candels and he bid me descend by some Stairs to the BASEMENT of the house.

As we descend'd further I was said beset by APPREHENSION as the light of the Candels did diminish and grate SHADOWS as if of Giants appear'd around us.

Do not be AFFEAR'D said Dr Swift. What is it to dismay us that we are but Littel BEASTS ourselves amongst the noblest of Giants. Then he stopt and, raisning the Candels, illuminated a corner of the room.

Look uponst this, he Instruct'd me, as it is my *Prize Exhibition* in my Cabinet of Curiousities.

Upon a Table there was a glass Bottle and in it were little creatures in the shape of Men. When they saw us they ran to the Side and, so insolently, did P___ onto the Glass forming tiny Rivers of p___ on the glass.

Prominent amongst them was a pair. The female was Hairy and Vulgar in dress and comportment. She seem'd to smile and turn'd to us and shew'd those Parts that hath but one Purpose for both beasts and men. When the male saw this he took out his PRIAPIC MEMBER which may have been enormous if it were not Small and proceed'd to Exercise it rigourously with both of his HANDS.

I cover'd my face that I might BLIND my eyes so as that I might see the Subject no longer.

Dr Blunt, he sade to me, have you never *Spent*?

At first I did not understand him. Then I took it for a Lewd and Base insulte and I berat'd him for Chiding a humble guest in his House.

Dr Blunt, you have an antique estimation of the propriety of Man. I ask you, if men could Squat and deliver hen's Eggs to the ground instead of Excrement would that make him more or less of a Beast?

I noted that he address'd me with a VEHEMENCE that made me quiver and shake In this *World Turn'd Upside Down* I was afear'd that my life itself would be Forfeit and my Soule would be set in Darknesse. I found my myself in a *Swoone* in which the Dr address'd me as if from a darke reverie.

> Swift. *Dr BLUNT, you are so blunt as I am as Sharp as a pikestaff. You are indeed Dr GULLIBLE and I shall name you such.*
> Blunt. *Dr Swift, I would have Chid'd you for so calling me, but my eyes cannot bear more of this contrary World. I pray you, let me be releas'd from this Place.*
> Swift. *Perhaps I should not do so as my Collection is onlie wanting of one Admission to be Complete; to whit, a DUNCE...*

⧗

I am Jonathan Blunt, God help me, of Fareham, in the Countie of Hampshire, and this is my Testament. Written in my mynd is the hideous LAUGHTER of Dr Swift as I expell'd myself at grate haste from his damned house lest I be confin'd there *in perpetuum*!

And where do I dwell now? In the vile Cofee-houses of the great Wen? In the far Scratches of Surrey? In the Bellie of the beast, in the folios of the Bestiarie, in the Hall of Looking-glasses? Among the Freaks of Bartholomew Fair? In the horrid lakes of *Pandæmonium*?

Imagine me, rather, in a grete Cavern where neither the light of the Moone or the Stars, or either of the Sun will penetrate. And there there are serpents and Spiders and all things that Creep and Crawle. And there too in poore Jonathan Blunt who keeps them as his onlie Friends, for he is a Monster among them all, and so created in the lighte of God's goodenesse, and he has been chosen to Know it. *Pata necesse est multa mortalem mala.*

HEARTLESS

[*Editor's note*] *I discovered this story, handwritten on folio lined paper, in the National Library of Congress in Autumn 1979. It was neatly folded and hidden between a volume of Peacock's* History of the American Indigenous Peoples *and Kelly's* Americana.

It is some time now since I awoke. It was in that part of Columbia known to the English as Dead Man's Garden—the sump where the rainforest ends, the land falls to a smelly sludgy morass and then rises to a more equitable scrubland where the tropical heat meets the cold drizzle from the mountain. Here it was that the forces of the government, in between their strenuous efforts to run the country, to establish a working parliament, build a hospital, sack a church, or erase the spirit of fear and superstition from the hearts of the people, engaged in countless petty skirmishes, farcical and sometimes bloody, with the sundry forces of the opposition—usually their own sort gone bad.

The local indians were somewhere on the periphery of this. As they knew the land better they could usually be relied on to serve the side of the government forces, but their loyalty was suspect, especially when there was no pay, and, anyway, the trivial brass luckpennies they were served by their masters had, as far as anyone could understand, only symbolic value to a people who eked their living from a harsh land. Worse still, they ate slugs, plucked hairs from their bodies, supped sickly nostrums and often went on strange excursions, leaving their bodies behind untended for a day or two days during which time they were useless as a fighting force.

When I awoke. I was stretched on a flat stone—around me a circle of painted indians. Although it did not surprise me at the time, it was odd that the moment they caught sight of me stirring, they fled. I was left alone in the hazy dusty air and the gathering dusk. I soon understood why this had occurred. I found an aluminium water bottle pierced by a bullet hole and in its shiny surface I examined my face. My skin was yellow and glossy, the cheekbones swollen and gross, the eyes sunken and red. I was the perfect candidate for a second-rate horror movie.

However, worse was to follow. Noticing that my canvas waistcoat was loose, I put my hand to my chest. In it was a round cavity. I put my fist into it. It came out covered with a disgusting yellow pus. There was no blood. A few flies hovered around my hand.

A military career teaches one to be stoical about life. I knew it was unusual for a man to survive when his heart had been removed, but for all that I quickly decided to be thankful for the smaller mercy and pursue the matter no further. Rather, I thought, I had to find my way back to some sort of civilisation. On examination, I decided that I was of Latin-American origin, although my natural tongue appeared to be English. A perusal of my possessions revealed that I was some sort of mercenary engaged in retaliatory warfare against government rebels. My fatigues were of a sickly brown hue stained with patches of darker brown. A scumpled log book in one pocket gave me a name—but it didn't appeal to me. Instead I compacted the few pages into a wad and sealed the hole in the canteen. I then filled it with sand. I inserted the object into the hole in my chest and sewed the wound together with a cactus spike and the khaki threads from my few rags. Surprisingly, the wound healed completely within a couple of days and I set about improving my appearance so that I could at least pass among the people of this country without inciting comment or courting blows.

Foolishly, I spent some time searching for my stolen heart, then I remembered, or thought I remembered, that in my last vision of the savages they seemed to have red cherubic lips.

🕱

And so, until this day, it has been a fairly solitary life. For some time I made a modest living from making and selling sisal ropes, at times I dealt quite successfully in a sticky and pungent brown substance extracted from coffee and, for a few years, I crewed on a tramp steamer around the Caribbean.

However, it came as something of a shock to me when I first came to the small town of C...ville in one of the mid-western states. In fact, for a bloodless creature accustomed to the equatorial zone the cold was more than a shock. I soon discovered that in a chilly wind or a winter's snow I had to remain at home well wrapped and protected. Otherwise, I would be caught outdoors and simply freeze, coming stiffly to a standstill, frozen to the spot until a few rays of sun or the heat of a streetlamp freed me enough to continue slowly on my way.

Nevertheless, my life has been pleasant enough here. I go to occasional social evenings and the people are unfailingly polite and affable. My strange condition neither appals or amuses them although sometimes they will make harmless wry comments like 'the iceman cometh' and 'don't shatter the mirror'. One reason, I think, that these ordinary people can be so unconcerned by my far from ordinary condition is that they are all far from perfect themselves. Sometimes, in fact, I suspect that they are all missing a part of themselves! But I never pursue the matter. I try to keep myself the best I can and contribute what little I can to the community.

I play chess twice a week with Dr C...r. He has made me come to understand that there are those more sorely afflicted than myself. Dr C...r once told me a story: When some cannibal tribes captured their enemy they would save one predestined man from the cooking pot. To stop him escaping they would cut off his arms and legs and, from then on, they would worship him for a year like a god, present him with feathers of the bird of paradise, fine foods and the handsomest of the village maidens. At the end of the year they would mock him, flog him and tear him to tiny pieces with their bare hands.

I realise that this story is only a joke, an apocrypha or a metaphor, but it comforts me all the same.

Recently, however, there has been a more disturbing development. Paper, as we know, is itself organic. It will last just as long as its constituents remain stable. Cheaper paper, high in cellulose, will deteriorate more quickly and more completely. My complexion has darkened, my skin is coarser. If I press my thumb or the ball of my hand into an arm or leg the impression stays there, like a dent in a beanbag.

I have a dream each night that I am floating on a sea of opaque white water. Miniature storm clouds cascade past inches from the tip of my nose. I cannot move. When I awake a filament blocks my nostrils and my ears, my lips are crusted and a film clouds my eyes. I need to pass water but it is too painful to contemplate.

⧖

My story, I know, is of no real consequence. We all meet misfortune at some time in our travels and I have been lucky enough to grow old. My only regret is that I have had two lives of which I can only recall one. But one should not yearn after what cannot be recovered. For now I am content to lie, well covered, in my bed and feverishly dream of sky and sea and desert.

EDITOR'S NOTE: Clearly this story is not meant to be taken literally. Dr C...r numbers among his patients several who have suffered traumas as a result of the Vietnam war, a handful of suicidal depressives, and one gentleman who periodically tries to persuade the police that he is a well-known Nazi war criminal.

ZUGSWANG

The chess-board is the world, the pieces are the phenomena of the universe, the rules of the game are what we call the laws of Nature. The player on the other side is hidden from us. We know that his play is always fair, just, and patient. But we also know, to our cost, that he never overlooks a mistake, or makes the smallest allowance for ignorance.

Thomas Henry Huxley

Dr Stauber is excited. He has risen before seven in his mews flat, breakfasted lightly and, too hurriedly, shaven his upper lip and the fringes of his elfin beard, staunching the blood with soap and a piece of waxed paper. He carefully irons his new satin shirt from Beauchamp & Co as he listens to the news on the radio of the escalating casualties in the Middle-Eastern war. Dr Stauber has a new neighbour and a visitor for lunch.

At 12.30 precisely, Kasprowicz, chess grandmaster and world title contender, knocks on Dr Stauber's door. He is of medium height, dusky complexion with short thinning hair and deep greyish eyes. He is dressed in neatly pressed jeans and a cashmere jumper.

⌛

They lunch on canapés Dr Stauber has ordered from his local delicatessen, potato rosti and chicken satay (Dr Stauber has checked that Kasprowicz has no religious or ethical objection to this menu). Their conversation varies widely. Kasprowicz talks with controlled passion of the erstwhile pogroms in his home country. They consider, as liberal and rational men, pragmatic solutions to the refugee crisis in the Gulf. Eventually they talk about chess—

about the skills and aptitude necessary to be a grandmaster, about the pressures of match play on the competitors.

Dr Stauber recalls a favourite aphorism: 'skill at chess is not a mark of a great intellect but of a great intellect gone wrong'. Kasprowicz laughs gently. 'I remember the words of Napier: 'life is not long enough for chess, but that is the fault of life, not of chess'!' Meanwhile, the mantel clock ticks the time away, and the silent radio leaves the continuing casualties of war unreported.

'On the other hand', Dr Stauber points out, didn't Shaw say that chess is a foolish expedient for making idle people believe they are doing something clever, when they are merely wasting their time'.

'Dear Dr Stauber, I'm afraid you may very well be right!' They share the joke like comrades in some fantastic enterprise that only they comprehend.

Later, they talk of literature, Of Eco, Borges and Calvino, Of stories told from tarot cards; of the infamous prince of Margaretenburg, who built a conceptual city of maps and words and etchings. At one point, Kasprowicz, who realises that he will retire from his chosen vocation before he is old, reveals his quixotic ambition to write a history of the world based only on the squares and pieces of the chessboard. Not only will all the famous battles of the past be encompassed there, but there will be little scenes of love, hate, betrayal. In the territory of the board. all human experience will be represented, appraised and recorded.

Finally, as the clock ticks toward the time of parting, Dr Stauber has a request for Kasprowicz.

'Before you go, my friend. could you do me a great favour. For five years now I have been playing a correspondence game with a colleague, a Dr Saunders in Wellington, New Zealand. Could you look at it for me?'

Kasprowicz, who normally has no use for the chessboard and its accoutrements, merely asks him to name the pieces and their squares. He sits with his eyes closed for several minutes and then demonstrates, to Dr Stauber's complete satisfaction, that it is, beyond reasonable doubt, a hopelessly lost game for white.

'However,' he adds, 'you need not take what I say too seriously, there are still many options. In this game alone there are more combinations than the number of atoms in the universe. In that respect, the infinity of the conceivable exceeds our useless attempts to represent the inconceivable.'

Dr Stauber is silent. He is thinking of the chessboard and of the sky and the stars. He remembers Marco Polo, who, playing chess with Kubla Khan, points out a single square of the board that is made from a different wood from the rest, a wood that was cut from the ring of a tree that was cut in a year of drought, with a knot formed from bud that had been born but then died in the frost of the night.

Dr Stauber thanks Kasprowicz profusely for his company. He hopes that they will meet again. As the grandmaster exits he remembers another quotation that he thinks may amuse the doctor. It is by H G Wells: 'there is no happiness in chess. It is a curse upon man.'

After Kasprowicz has departed, Dr Stauber switches on the six-o-clock news. He goes to his chessboard. It has been a busy day and he had thought of many things. Of war, and the words of great men long since dead, and of the earth and the sky. He selects the pieces, one by one, carefully and deliberately in order of their seniority, pawns to king, one white for one black piece, and deposits them in the wastepaper basket under his desk. When he has finished, he closes the chessboard along the central hinge, with a thud. The finality has the ring of a good book, thoroughly read.

Later he will write a short letter, but, for now, he wishes to contemplate the inscrutability of the universe and the folly of man.

NOW IS THE DISCOUNT OFF OUR WINTER TENTS

Sous la glace où calme il repose,
Oh! qui pourra fondre ce coeur!
Oh! qui pourra mettre un ton rose
Dans cette implacable blancheur!

Théophile Gautier

Now is the discount off our winter tents

Advertising slogan, Blacks of Greenock

Now is the discount off our winter tents,
Anoint the feet of thy frosty boots,
Summer is icumen forty winters.
Odds like that were never meant to last.

In the morning I came to the station. There were two entrances but both were secured by automatic barriers that kept out the wind and most of the cold. There was a coffee stall and I ordered some tea which was served by a woman in fingerless gloves and a hand-knitted bobble hat. She smiled at me. She had nice teeth but her eyes were unfocused and I realised that she was, or would rather have been, somewhere else.

It was that time when the diminishing settled silence of the night was occasionally punctured by an unexpected sound—the clanking of a train uncoupling, the hiss of a tea urn, even the tap tap of a blind man's cane and the ruffle of his guide dog scratching his leg—until it was absorbed again and a sluggish sleepiness oozed back over the scene.

I got on the train and chose a window seat with a table on the left, facing forward. I looked around. At the top door of the carriage, I could just make out a man standing on the platform with a suitcase gesticulating to—and perhaps arguing with—the guard. Suddenly, he turned on his heels and walked back towards the gate.

At the end of the carriage at the diagonally opposite table seat to me was a tall gaunt man in a dark anorak sitting practically motionless, his head tilted a little towards the window. Further down the carriage and also facing me, sat an elderly lady dressed in a buttoned-up coat and a woolly hat. She looked anxious and she was quite forcefully and repetitively rolling the fingers of one hand in the other.

My eyes were almost closing when suddenly I was jerked backwards. The brakes were off and the engine of the train engaged with the wheels to slowly move it forwards with, it seemed, such as effort that each axle strained to reach its apex before the relief of falling away to the ground. The wheels ground against the rails and, at each turn, gained a little momentum.

I had boarded the train within the city but soon it had chugged out to the river estuary and the shadow of the hills traced themselves against the dawning sky. I was so concentrating on my own journey.

Then, I was jerked from my reverie when the ticket inspector appeared. He was a small man, balding but with notable sideburns.

'The ticket office was closed…', I said.

Then he added, 'Ire or Dismay? Single or Return?'

'Single', I said, '… and eh…' I was unsure.

He looked exasperated. 'I'll give you a return. There is no difference in the cost.' He looked me up and down. 'Ire, I suspect. You don't look like Dismay.' He leaned towards me as if offering a confidence. 'The lady three seats up', he said, 'now that is a classic case of Dismay.'

I felt uncomfortable, so I tried to strike up some conversation. 'You aren't too busy this morning?'

'Not especially, but we are coupling up with a carriage of Calamity at Crianlarich. We'll see then.'

Something just came into my head. 'I saw a gentlemen before. He didn't seem to get on the train.'

'Yes, he had a valid ticket but we couldn't let him on. Special reason. Spruceness. Couldn't allow that on the train.'

⧖

I descended from the train at a lonely station at the edge of a moor. The carriage had missed the platform and I had to jump ankle deep into soft fresh snow. I watched the train recede into the distance before I began to trudge up the mountain as the sun was setting.

When I reached the suitable final spot and settled, I took the top off the flask and swallowed the whisky-flavoured liquid. It was bitter. Then I remembered the chocolate bar I had bought on the train—half remained in my pocket. I cracked the two wafers apart and chewed them in small bites. Then I washed the fragments down with the contents of the flask, stinging the gums between my teeth, until it was drained to the end. There was a gust of wind and a small flurry of snow flakes. I tucked my mitted hands under my armpits. In the distance, the last of the winter sun was setting behind the jagged ridge. Was it as beautiful as I had expected? I felt nothing but the acid in my stomach and a light in my forehead that refused to go out no matter how tightly I closed my eyes.

⧖

It was morning! Ruddy rods of the rising sun flickered on my eyelids. To my astonishment I opened my eyes a little and an orange rose pressed into my forehead.

It was some time before I could move anything but my eyelids. Then, in a jerky fashion I found myself clenching my fists. My frozen Dachstein mitts bent and cracked. I removed the mitts and rubbed my hands together, rolling the fingers of one hand on the other. A reminder of the old lady on the train flashed into my head. Dismay. There was no warmth but there was an absence of pain.

There was nothing to do but to return to that station. When I had sat the cold lump of my body down, the ticket collector appeared.

He looked at the ticket and at me. 'It's a return', he said.

'Yes,' I said, 'of course. You sold it to me. 'He shook his head. 'Oh no,' he said, 'not me. Perhaps one of my brothers. I have many brothers…'

I alighted at the station in the city and wandered dull wet streets stirred by gusting winds. My legs were weary and my feet sore by the time I reached the bank of tenements on the hill; black and craggy, winding into a sky of leaden grey clouds. A biting rain blew into the back of my trouser legs. I looked up as the sky began to crack into grey and black and white. The tenements were cleft into buttressed walls and gloomy closes. There was no longer anything left that conformed to my own memory: no expected number, no welcoming home.

Retracing my steps with the rain still drenching my knee caps and stinging my face, I came to some traffic lights and a row of shops. There was a cafe in the traditional Italian style and a man in an apron, who I assumed was the proprietor, standing outside.

'Come on in,' said the cafe owner. 'Have some tea. Put your boots in the corner and dry your trousers and socks by the radiator. Everybody does.'

He looked me up and down. 'If you need the facilities,' he added, 'there is a large key by the door, and they are entered via the adjacent close. It has always been like that.'

He was small, with greying sideburns and a trimmed moustache. I thought I recognised him. He looked at me and smiled. 'I have many brothers', he said.

I sat there as my clothes began to dry. Various customers came and left. All seemed to be greeted with a mug of tea by the owner. Periodically, the customers arose and went back and forth through a door at the back of the cafe. One old lady and a tall man looked familar. The others were all sorts, old and young, but they all seemed to sit quietly on their own.

I called over the cafe owner. 'I do recognise you, don't I', I said.

'That is not uncommon', he said. 'Some think I am a relative, some think I am a character in a novel by a well-known Glasgow author.'

'I do not have any relatives', I said, 'and I'm not familiar with any Glasgow novels.'

He looked at me in a manner that reminded me of a schoolteacher. 'I see,' he said. 'Perhaps there are some books on our bookcase you could read. Do not despise the narratives of literature', he said. 'One day you may have the privilege to serve in those yourself.'

He beckoned to the door at the back of the cafe. 'Now come with me.'

He pulled at the handle but it did not open the door. 'You see,' he took my own hand and laid it on the handle, 'this door will only open for you.'

He was right. I pulled the door open and we stepped inside.

The room was small and very specifically laid out. It was in the form of the alcove where I slept in my childhood room and kitchen. There was the plaster Supercar plaque I had painted myself on the wall, the little night light that stayed on to keep away the bogeymen that lived behind the curtains, the Batman and the Justice League of America comics that I read on the mahogany sideboard. And there was the bed where I lay sometimes at night counting to one hundred time after time in my head to stay awake until my father came home from the two to ten shift.

'This is for you', he said. 'It is what you wanted?' He shrugged.
I didn't say anything.

'You will fit in well enough here', he said. 'In time maybe you could arrange a quiz or poetry readings or something. The regulars would like that…'

⧗

As the day wore on, I could not resist periodically checking the view from the café door. The weather changed, growing darker and lighter. Sometimes the mountain appeared at the bottom of the street, clothed in different seasons. I didn't really recognise it any more.

Later, I sat with my mug of tea as the clouds formed, darkened and then broke in the sky. I was waiting, but I didn't know what for.

USHER

It is buried in the past. An eternity of times ago. I recall it the day that the new life began for me and the old one grew, (I can envisage still, though as a remnant of memory) into fiction. Less of a fact as a dogma, the strange sound of the wine glass if you circulate a finger damp with a heavystaining in a just so manner around the rim. Memories, you see, have the same effect on me— they play on some sympathetic string. I am shrill. I am vibrato.

It began with the darkness. The city in which I lived at that time was beset with dampness and gloom. Like the others I struggled on each day in a vain pretence at what may be called a normal life, but slowly, very slowly, so slowly as to be almost imperceptible, one thing began to change—the darkness came.

Day by day the nights grew longer and the days became shorter. Nature, if such a thing still exists, dictates the change of the seasons—but this was no season, it had the inevitability and finality of forever.

Each evening I had been accustomed to seeing from the small round fenestra in my room the dusk made ruddy by the coaly glow from the steelmakers that encompassed the east side of the city. Now it came to pass that the lights went out—the city settled into a glove of darkness.

Yet I could have withstood this dark sentence if it had not been for one thing—one nagging doubt. Without the walls of my sequestered lodgings everyday affairs went on in much the same manner as before the Uptowners gathered in their glass porches and hunted the heavens for distant suns, the Downtowners pickled their insides in Bull's Blood and marched in procession from the factory doors with banners proclaiming 'It is Hopeless' and 'Close the Furnace Now'.

The horrifying thought came to me that perhaps I was the only one inflicted by this terrible blight. That I was out of synchronisation with the rest. That this twilight beast was an inhabitant only of my personal universe.

This idea so influenced me that I soon fell prey to a strange wasting ill—I could feel my flesh receding, my blood thickening in the veins so that in the process of time, I imagined, it would distill itself into small red crystals and I would clatter to the floor in an avalanche of rubies

Luckily, this malady now confined me, alone, to my small sparse room. I had for some time previously employed my credits usefully to collect. I read a great deal at that time—a limited but tasteful library. Though the short thick tallow by my bed grew dimmer by the day. It was my only consolation and favourite lines —'Tyger! Tyger! Burning Bright', 'Margaret, Art Thou Grieving', 'When Lilace Last In The Dooryard Bloomed And The Great Star Early Drooped In The Western Sky In The Night'— whispered in my head for days—or nights.

Then one time I was perusing a volume of the collected works of Poe and came upon that passage in the strange story of the family of Usher in which Roderick succumbs to the terror:

I must perish in this deplorable folly. thus, thus, and not otherwise, shall I be lost. I dread the events of the future, not in themselves, but in their results. I shudder at the thought of any, even the most trivial incident, which may operate upon this intolerable agitation of soul.

I have, indeed, no abhorrence of danger, except in its absolute effect—in terror. In this unnerved, in this pitiable condition, I feel that the period wiil sooner or later arrive when I must abandon life and reason together, in some struggle with the grim phantasm, FEAR.

I had read these lines many times before but on this occasion my nerve also, stretched taut by my infirmity, snapped. The walls around me seemed to reverberate and echo PEAR, FEAR, PEAR.

The dampness consolidated into running tears. The feathery mould errupted into diaphanous tendrils to clutch at my hands and my legs. Looking down at the yellowed pages of the volume I saw the symmetrical preserved pressed carcase of a small spider ingrained into the paper.

Of course, I had no choice from that moment but to give myself up to the realms of poetic fiction. Concentrating my attention on the fading far wall of my room I believed I could detect a small section of darkened walnut—of the type used to panel the library of the House of Usher.

After some days (or hours or minutes) at this exercise the image compacted in texture and detail and grew to occupy the greater part of my limited vista.

Baumgartner, in his memoirs, recalls his time as an Alpinist in the Grandes Jorasses in which an especially severe avalanching had preserved and rendered intact to the rescue party six perfectly frozen corpses. After being deposited on the church floor overnight the small heat of the candles and suchlike had effected such a notable thawing on these unfortunate gentlemen that each dead shell had risen slowly during the night to welcome their rescuers in the morning sitting bolt upright. Such, it seems was the method by which I rose on that day to discover that my dream had grown into reality. Now at last I could run my finger down the vellum of the volumes in the library of Usher.

They were all there Machiavelli's *Belphegor*, Swedenborg's *Heaven and Hell*, the *City of Sun* by Campanella, D'Indagine's *Chiromancy* and, of course the *Mad Trist* of Lancelot de Canning. I could feel the embossing, scan the print, crimp the pages. This domain was now, by order of possession, my own.

☒

Although, of necessity, I write with the advantage of hindsight, it is essential that I should explain that at first I had no idea why it had been chosen that I should be within these walls or indeed whether this was the home of my imagining or, in fact, the real home of the Ushers. But who else with whom I could claim not even a nodding acquaintance could possess such a place—gaunt, dark, constituting both a peak and a peninsular. Above all imposing but yet unseen as it was obvious from the prospect of the few windows that I could expect no visitors. Moreover, I had realised almost instantly, within the compass of a very few years, that the house was constructed neatly on an infinite geometrical figure such that the sides continued round in a fourth dimension.

Thus, as in the undulations of Einsteinian space or the folding of the insidious computer screen, to exit from any room at the east of the house would only ensure entry to another room at the west symmetrically arranged around a central point. Therefore, although I did not know exactly how many rooms were to be found in the house (as there were many and some were identical) I was aware that they constituted a finite number and that was comforting as I passed daily between its membranous cells.

How I could weary myself, if I had time, by recalling the details of my new abode. Suffer me to insist that a mere precis will suffice:

Many of the rooms were libraries in which the shelves revolved on a central axis—turning the others like giant literary cogwheels (within the space of ten or twelve years I had inspected all the volumes).

Other rooms seemed dedicated to one solitary enigma—a beetle in a block of aspic that shone gold in the light of a candle, a stuffed black cat wanting one eye, a gesso mural of figures engaged in a satanic dance around the chamber. As I investigated further and descended to the vaults my finds grew more recondite.

In one, between the black blocks that rose in increasing mass to monolithic blackness, I entered a passage where I saw dangling above me bare human feet (I could not discern whether they were alive or dead).

In another of the vaults I detected a bottle-shaped pit with a vast blade suspended in Damoclean fashion above the centre.

In another, hands and forearms of stone as thick as Medusa's hair protuded from the walls.

In another, a series of arches radiated different colours (to pass through each registered a different emotion—so that one moment I would be shuddering with pity and the next aghast with shame). In another, a volume, bound in pigskin, the letters appearing in white on a perfect black background.

Eventually, as was inevitable, I found the central chamber. Above I could discern the firings of great furnaces and the dripping of molten metals. It was circular, with floor and ceiling painted black and smooth, with recesses round the walls. Seated in the centre was a figure clothed in the guise of hooded death.

The figure was in the form of a doppelganger of myself lost in a suspension between life and death. Eventually, after a passage of time encompassing an almost infinite number of other possibilities, I related to the figure a transcription of some of the mysterious words from the black book. The figure fell to dust (I noted, with disappointment, that my own mortal frame had not ceased to exist) revealing a staircase descending spirally in the centre of the floor and my mind and body were at once taken up by an intense, frantic, yet barely discernable whispering that chilled my fingertips, shivered my spine, and curdled my very breath.

It had been a period of unmeasurable time as I descended the staircase during which the air grew damper and thicker squeezing the breath from my lungs. There was, periodically, a momentary relief then it resumed the same inexorable grip. The paltry atmosphere squirted around my skull and caused my pressured brain a little more pain. But nothing could avert my attention— not from the absolute pain of descent but from the immediate more insufferable buzzing, the teasing feather of sound that vibrated through the tunnels of my nerves.

When I reached the origin there was no instant easing but merely the gradual seeping of some sense resembling reason and vaguely stirring my surroundings until the chamber was revealed.

A soft but untraceable aura of light invaded the chamber. The sound had softened to a single, regular but inerasable beating emanating from a casket that seemed to exude no light and was only visible, paradoxically, by its seeming absence.

When I opened the casket I found and held in the steady palm of my hand the beautiful but terrible source of the sound—a crystal glowing red in the perfect shape of a human heart.

At once I realised and reached—as if in a slumber— automatically to the pit of my breast whereupon I found a Daliesque drawer. It slid open with a well-oiled motion and therein I placed the vagrant gem.

THE SNARK *WAS* A BOOJUM

They roused him with muffins—they roused him with ice
They roused him with mustard and cress—
They roused him with jam and judicious advice
They set him conundrums to guess.

Lewis Carroll

Laertes Lebrun, the great French detective, sat silently resolutely applying a very special pomade to his moustaches with a fine-toothed tortoiseshell comb. Here he was ensconced alone in his room at Cathay, the country house of the Cholmondeley family, a various estate of sundry pieces that glowed vaguely in that limbo of opulence and indecision that Lebrun knew was what he saw as perpetually English. But this was not the Lebrun of yesteryear. Aged, enfeebled, inflicted with or affecting an infirmity that severely restricted his mobility and confined him for the best part to a cumbersome bath chair. When Wisden, the English country doctor and old friend of Lebrun, arrived after such a long absence from his erstwhile companion, he would be shocked: the hairs of Lebrun's moustaches had bolted—suddenly they were quite cadaverously white.

There was no doubt that at Cathay the Cholmondeley family were accommodating in the care of their guests. There were the simple pleasures of English country life applied with a panache that had once appealed to Lebrun. The finest nuances of his taste were catered for. In the morning when he arose, there sat attendant on him a bowl of warmed, slightly salted water and a dish containing some white powder for cleaning his teeth. In the evening before he retired a bowl containing exactly three tablespoons of olive oil—which he favoured for the care of his moustaches—sat upon a steel tripod heated by a single smokeless blue paraffin flame. In the patio the chaise longue was arranged at an angle that pleased him as he sat nourished by the mid morning sun. All things leaned towards convenience—and yet for Lebrun at that time, there was no commodité. An ultimate cariness assaulted him.

At seven o'clock the manservant came to enquire his pleasure.

'Port or claret, Monsieur Lebrun?'

'Claret, if you please, *un soupcon'*. Lebrun replied.

Medoc, St Emilion or Graves, Monsieur?'

Medec.

Pauilac, Margaux, Saint-Julian or Cantenac, Monsieur ?

Pauilac.'

'Chateau Lafite, Chateau Latour, Chateau Mouton-Rothschild, Chateau Pichon-Lalande, Monsieur

'Chateau Lafite, s'il vous plait.'

'Nineteen-seventeen, nineteen-eighteen or nineteen-nineteen?'

'I will have the seventeen. Merci!!'

Lebrun's soul signed with a misery at this capricious test of his discrimination. It was a strange design that condemned him to this—that his life revolved around an eternal series of increasingly refined choices. Lebrun felt totally divorced from his fate—as if some enigmatic god had imposed this life upon him. The insistent questions, the endless quest towards some catharsis of perfection. He had once thought that he understood the pattern to probe the mysteries of life. The Puzzle, the Quest, the Shaping, the Solution. Flurries of little grey cells endlessly reforming themselves to an infinitely complex formula until the moment of joy—the exact configuration! The key to fit the lock. The mystery *unlocked*. Was the art of the detective like this? Some sequence of discrete choices. Perhaps it was so. He had always taken the right road, always pared the filament of truth from the body of fiction or fancy. Always, until now! And now the weight of age and infirmity and experience held him down.

⧗

Lebrun was old. He was not, however, moribund. There was nothing deathly in his thoughts. He who had delved so often into the consequences and ramifications of death had come at this age to some impasse. Now for the first time he was uncertain. He was unnerved by the final mystery. As never before he was in expectation of something other than a meaningless vacuum beyond the veil.

Lebrun was old, but he had not lapsed into indifference. Lebrun the pristine philosopher did not quite know why he was here, suspended in this place, and yet for Lebrun the Detective there could be only one unavoidable purpose. Lebrun, the greatest detective of this or any other age, could only be here at Cathay to solve some mystery! However, if this was so then there was an inconsistency. Lebrun knew of no crime committed at Cathay—although the place had an aura about it, perhaps the ghost of some evil act that had taken place there. If there had been a crime committed there were no suspects—Lebrun could not remember meeting any of the guests or the staff at Cathay apart from the manservant who tended him. The mystery was more recondite than any he had ever known for this time there was no crime, no suspect, no prognosis, no solution. This time he was asked not only to solve the conundrum but to *postulate the question itself.* The starting point, he realized, must be the clues. There must be clues and clues upon clues—for any vestige of experience or reality could be a clue. The best clues, of course, were those that were never titled as such that passed idly by as footnotes to the great text. Lebron, of course, had the touch that delivered these insubstantial pieces of the puzzle. Hopefully, he could redeem himself and unearth enough shards to reconstruct the whole piece, and finish the job.

Lebrun searched, and Lebrun found clues—almost with ease. In each of the several rooms some enigma seemed to present itself. In one a chessboard set correctly for the game but with one piece missing—the king's pawn black. In another a singular coincidence startled him—a dark red blotch on a desk blotter seemed to conform to a perfectly symmetrical image of his own moustaches. In the pink room he noticed side by side, between Watt's *Latin Grammar* and a home counties gazetteer, two copies of *De Nugis Curialium* by Gualteri Mapes, edited by Thomas Wright, similar in composition but different imprints.

The task was tedious but Lebrun persisted until he revealed the lacuna of the first of volumes set against the second. The single sentence read: *And these insubstantial beings are of a nature betwixt Man and Angel and cannot, by dint of their own constitution, succeed to the House of their Maker.* Not the words but the tone of the passage brought a sudden chill to Lebrun's composure. Eventually, in the green lounge, Lebrun found something that seemed to him a singular oddity. A book of verse open at a page of the poem 'The Hunting of the Snark' by Lewis Carroll. At the top of the page was scrawled in red ink "The Five Unmistakable Marks of the Snark'. Glancing through the poem he noted the five unmistakable marks:

1. was its taste (which was meagre and crisp);
2. was its slowness in taking a jest;
3. was its fondness for bathing machines;
4. was its habit of getting up late.

The fifth and final unmistakable mark of this strange beast was inexorably deleted from the leaf in black Indian ink. No amount of scratching could reveal that fatal clue.

The setting of the sun that evening passed by unnoticed by Lebrun, engaged as he was in his labours. Reluctantly he called his ruminations to a halt for that day. Wisden would arrive that night but his aged comrade would retire before then. He decided to spend a half-hour before his night-cap to pen a letter to his friend. He concluded:

> My very dear Wisden, it has been so long. I hope that my short summary of the enigma that is presented to us will stimulate your curiosity. Finally, I say to you two things that you may think on tonight. Firstly, I hope that you have met our friend the waiter. Secondly, consider the conclusion of the poem of the snark—*mais en Francais!* A very good night and may le Bon Dieu preserve you until the morning, my dear Doctor.
>
> Your true friend,
Laertes Lebrun.

Lebrun knew that amongst all the confusion and uncertainty he was close to an answer. His old bones knew the feeling too well. Wisden, his old friend and confidant, would arrive in the morn and would be faced with a revelation. Objectively projecting his intellect outwith himself, Lebrun prepared to wait calmly for the outcome, curious in anticipation of the concluded labours of those tiny grey cells that he had always lauded. They were his private army, peopling his private universe—each living and dying on an impulse. They would come good. To each problem there was a solution. Thus he retired to a feverish sleep.

In the morning much had changed. No one attended Lebrun that morning at Cathay. His fever had resolved to a pallid mask that hid untold woes. He knew that he was obliged to outline the concluding details of the puzzle to his friend Wisden. After the accepted pleasantries, this he did in his usual concise but teasing fashion.

'And now, mon cher ami. I see from your baffled expression that it is necessary for me to elucidate.' Lebrun composed himself but some may have detected a shift in his usual confident posture.

'You must understand that my reluctance is simply because the truth may be painful to you as it is to me.'

'Nevertheless, it is the truth.'

There was a taut silence for a moment.

'The truth, my dear friend, began to come through to me last night with a sudden realization. It was this. I the great Laertes Lebrun, was weary. Not only weary, but I was struck with a strong sense of futility! There seemed no end to the thankless task I had assigned myself to decipher the clues I had discovered in my seeming eagerness.

'Mon ami, ambition, it is the fifth mark of the wretched snark. I, Laertes Lebrun, was too ambitious. It was when I abandoned my beloved logic and relied instead on my intuition that the solution came.'

Lebrun paused, almost as if to ascertain that the pieces did fit before revealing the inevitable.

Think, Wisden. 'The Hunting of the Snark'—it is what you call in English the nonsense poem. It is exactly that—it makes no sense. Do you not see! The impossible snark, the bibliographical importunities of Monsieur Wright, they were, how do you say it... what you call it... the red herring! We were, how do you say it, duped. I, the great Laertes Lebrun, the finest detective of all time, was fed like a goose!

'And yet, if you think of it, my friend, what is the red herring! It does not exist in real life. It is a product of fiction for it presupposes an intention to deceive—the device of the omnipotent author!

'To deceive or to tease. The missing chess piece—I was a pawn in this game, of course. The blemished blotter that parodied my own moustaches. But the solution, my dear Wisden, was in none of this. It was to be found in some thing much smaller.'

Lebrun sighed; a long deep sigh that billowed in the terse air with all the desperation of his perhaps non-existent soul. The realization came upon him that his last case, his final answer, was his greatest triumph—but the solution was harsh and bitter and afforded him little pleasure.

My dear Wisden,' he recommenced, but Wisden was no longer there. "The solution is in the *cedilla*! I asked you, you remember, to look at the end of the nonsense poem. *mais en Francais*! You remember the end. Where the silly creatures are hunting everywhere for the baker:

> They hunted till darkness came on, but they found
> > Not a button, or feather, or mark,
> By which they could tell that they stood on the ground
> > Where the Baker had met with the Snark.

Here are the notes you yourself have scribbled, my friend. *Ils ont cherché ca et la...* Your French, of course, like all the English, is intolerably clumsy, but it is sufficient to see the point—*Ce n'est pas ca*! I, Laertes Lebrun, master of many tongues, asked him for *un soupcon,* and he in his imperfect tongue replied to me *un soupcon,* Monsieur! Lebrun paused to gain a faltering breath.

"The humble cedilla. A small thing but conspicuous by its absence. And why... ?'

Lebrun cast his eyes around him for a cue, but there was none.

'It is the English typewriter—a crude instrument at best—it has not the cedilla!'

'Do you not see? Our words are merely these inconsequential markings on a sheet. We are ourselves a fiction! Creations of another's imagination!'

Lebrun was all alone now in a vacuum. The greatest detective that was ever in creation had, as he was fated to do, solved the great enigma—the ultimate problem of his own existence. He reflected that there was no choice. It had been inevitable that before his end he would fathom these depths—otherwise would never have been created; for as much a part of his make-up as his moustaches, his fastidious concern for order, was his *infallibility*. Lebrun had never failed. He had been teased all along but he had not been defeated.

However, there was no choice now—as it had been all along, As much as anyone he was a prisoner of his own created self. The weariness in his bones no longer troubled him. His infirmity was a pretence of a kind—the artist's final chiaroscuro. Now, his was the fate of Carroll's baker: to out in mid breath with the hint of a cry a futile last gasp for his individual existence,

Now? There was a great variety of poisons and mediums. Mere water now, he knew, could act as arsenic blessed by the flashing rod of fictional ghost—the philosopher's stone that could transmute lead into gold, transfigure bread into flesh, pen reality into fiction. But that was not the chosen road and, reflecting gratefully that there were no more decisions after this one, Lebrun straightened his posture, carefully lifted the pistol the gracious curve of which had automatically been drawn in his right hand, determined to take pleasure in his last eternal moment in this sphere of his existence, and almost silently, shot a hole neatly, with careful symmetry, in the centre of his forehead.

STORY CUT SHORT

I will be brief. For some time I was employed in a medical capacity at the Sante prison. My role was to ascertain and testify to the death of those lost souls who encountered Madame La Guillotine. (You may think that, in view of their certain end, my presence was hardly necessary; but, as you will see, the pathology of decapitation is more complex than generally imagined).

At 5.30 am, on the twenty-eight of June 1905, I was privileged to be able to conduct an unusual experiment on the murderer Languille. With the agreement of the prisoner, I was allowed to address the capitis. Immediately after the blade had fallen, the eyelids and lips contracted for some five seconds, then the face relaxed, leaving only the white of the conjunctiva visible. Then, there was no doubt, the felon's eyes fixed on mine. I called his name: 'Languille!'. He blinked several times in response. This lasted for about 40 seconds then gradually eased until he was motionless.

For several years I conducted these experiments, increasing their sophistication. I devised a device that, attached to the ears, swung the head upside down, thus preventing the spurt of blood from the jugular foramer and extending consciousness. All this time I never saw a face that seemed to exhibit pain or horror. Some rolled their eyes or tried to mouth words. The wicked Landru, subject of my penultimate experiment (who had refused to hear the mass or take a last glass of brandy), I swear, winked at me insolently and remorselessly.

Now I was in the rapture of obsession. I began to think of the moments following decapitation as almost a joyous relief, an escape from corporal and visceral servitude. a moment unpolluted with consequences, a time for contemplation before meeting the one true maker. I thought of the theory that, at the moment just before death, one's whole life is lived again, but more perfectly. The axe or bullet slow to a stop and devout souls have time to recite their sweetest prayers and make their peace with the corruptible world. I had read that some of the pygmy tribes of Africa, who beheaded their enemies, compassionately attached their heads to a springy sapling so that their last moments seemed like a transport to heaven. Thoughts like these tormented me. I pondered day and night on the same questions. I needed to know.

⌛

I devised the machine and nailed the upside down clock to the wall. The trip was set so that, when I released the blade, the stringed device would hold the head in the exact position.

So, now at last I know! The lapse between decapitation and death is at least 54 seconds—just enough time for me to recount this extraordinary...

RYMOUR BOOKS

poetry · history · debate